BLOOD VENGEANCE

by
Dan L. Faulkner

4-7-17

To Dana,
Hope You EnJoY
iT "wingman"!

Dan Faulkner

DORRANCE
PUBLISHING CO
EST. 1920
PITTSBURGH, PENNSYLVANIA 15238

Dorrance Publishing Co
585 Alpha Drive
Suite 103
Pittsburgh, PA 15238
Visit our website at *www.dorrancebookstore.com*

ISBN: 978-1-4809-3735-2
eISBN: 978-1-4809-3758-1

This book is dedicated to all those who have suffered a traumatic brain injury. May their lives be full of purpose.

Dan L. Faulkner

Acknowledgments

Thanks to Tish Hand for her encouragement and editing prowess.

1

In the musty basement of the Longtree Pawnshop in Ulm, Montana, a chess game was taking place between two ex-cons.

Chris Fields, at 6'1", 230 pounds, was not a man you wanted to meet in a dark alley. In his 35 years, he relied on his fists and muscular build, after two years in prison in Washington state for burglary with Lamar Singleton.

Lamar, an African-American, at 33, tall and lean, relied on his mouth for talking his way out of trouble, or getting into it.

Chris, in a blue t-shirt, faded jeans, and trademark python boots, was trying to teach Lamar the game of chess. "No, the knight can't move like that, a-hole. It moves in an 'L' shape. Two in any direction and one square over - like this."

Stroking his moustache, Lamar said, "I'll put my money on black, white boy."

"Then I would suggest you learn how to play the game like David does. He puts his soul into it."

"Man, he has no soul, and the proof is in this stupid plan of his." Lamar adjusted his bib overall shoulder strap, which was always loose, like his mouth.

At the top of the stairs stood the man, David Samuel Longtree. At 37, a short 5'10", with black hair in a ponytail, 190 pounds, the only thing long on him was a penchant for crime. He came from a long line of ancestors who preferred staying in the shadows. His grandfather ran whiskey for the Chicago mob in the '20s and '30s, only to be shot dead running from the police. His father died in prison after a bank robbery attempt in South Dakota when David was only 10 years old. Currently his older brother, Carl, was serving 20 years at Waupon State Prison in Wisconsin for bank robbery and shooting a security guard.

"You calling me stupid, you fucking road apple?" he asked in a low but firm voice.

"No, no, it's just…just…"

"Just what? If you don't like it here, leave," Longtree replied, walking down the stairs.

"I'll do whatever you ask, but man, we need to think this through some more."

"Leave the thinking to me, understand? Chris, make me some coffee, and make it strong and black."

Fields shot Singleton a dirty look. "Not a problem," he said, heading up the stairs, sidestepping David with his head down.

Reaching the bottom, David eyed Lamar cringing in his seat. "Don't crap your pants, and never touch that chess set. That's expensive ivory, more than you're worth. That set was owned by the great Paul Morphy, U.S. chess champion in 1859."

Lamar shuddered. "I'm sorry, man. It was that white boy's idea upstairs."

Just then David's intrusion detection system went off. He checked the camera monitor. It was Tracy Burke.

"Get off your ass and let Montana's best little prostitute in," David said.

Tracy was a young student using prostitution to earn extra money at Missoula College when David found her for sex three years ago. Even now, at 33, she still looked like a little reddish-blond-haired schoolgirl. He liked the gold hoop earrings, matching suede boots and jacket. She was a part-time secretary at a used car dealer by day, a high-class call girl by appointment only by night.

Chris brought down a pot of coffee and some cups, followed by Tracy and Lamar moments later.

"Why does it smell down here? Have you guys been pissing in the sump-pump drain again?" she asked. She reached into her Versace purse and pulled out a digital disk that she made. Looking at David, she said, "Hey, sweet cheeks, here's the disk on Gregory, that submissive bastard."

"Excellent, my sweet. Do we have him where we want him?" he asked with a grin.

"By the short hairs, my darling."

"Give that lady whatever she wants to drink," he said.

Chris and Lamar high-fived each other. She took a slow bow. "I would like to thank you all," she said with a Southern Texas accent. "I'll take a coffee, black with sugar."

"Let's remember that's only phase one. We still have to convince this bank president he has no choice in the matter," David said.

"That should be easy, with him taking it up his chute and wanting to be spanked all night long," she said.

"That sure brings back memories of prison, hey, Lamar?" Chris said, poking him in the chest.

"I never and you know it," Lamar said, slapping his hand away.

"Sometimes I think you both belong back there," David said.

After they both were released from prison, they met Longtree at a lowlife bar outside of Seattle two years ago. With no place to go, they decided to take him up on his offer of returning to Montana with him. Working at the pawnshop, they could keep a low profile and satisfy their parole officer. In them both, David found the perfect combination of street smarts and guts. Both were expendable to Longtree. But he used them to suit his own purpose: Lamar to set up appointments for Tracy and grunt work and Chris for the use of force if need be.

Glancing at the monitor once again, David said, nodding his head and rubbing his hands, "Here comes the boy now. Tracy, if you would, please," making a gesture to let him in.

"Now we get down to business," David said, taking a seat at a large old oak table the others were seated at.

2

"Why did you want to meet here, of all places, on a Sunday morning? It's not even nine A.M.," said Gregory Cameron.

"Probably afraid he'll miss church," Fields said, laughing, holding the disk up so everyone could see. Longtree could only smirk and shake his head back and forth.

"My wife will wonder where I am," Gregory said. He felt like throwing up at the dankness that invaded his nose as he made his way slowly down the stairs, holding onto the railing. At 58 years old and a large 245 pounds, he was slow and pudgy. "Why are we going down here? Who owns this place? Answer me."

Seductively, Tracy said, "Take my hand, sweetie. You'll see in a moment."

Gregory saw the three—Longtree, Fields, and Singleton—sitting at a large, worn oak table. "Good morning," he said as he took out a handkerchief to keep his stomach from turning from the latest smell of piss and moldy dampness.

"Take a squat," David said as he gestured towards a chair at the table.

"Man, look at the jowls on this dude. A Prada suit, Rolex watch, Italian silk tie. You'd think he's going to a funeral," Lamar said.

"Shut up," David said, making eye contact with Lamar.

"Do I know you gentlemen?" Gregory asked as he furrowed his dark eyebrows.

"I am David Longtree, owner of this establishment. You already know Tracy." He watched her move behind him to put her hands around his waist. "This is Chris and Lamar, my associates," David said, removing Tracy's hands. "Take a seat, Tracy."

Sitting next to David, she said, "Here's your man, if you can call him that."

Even though he was seated, Gregory felt his legs would go out from under him. "What's going on here?"

"Here's what it amounts to, fat boy. Do you remember having sex with Miss Tracy a week or so ago?" David asked.

"What business is it of yours?"

"Again with the questions," Chris said, flexing his fingers for a possible punch.

Gregory started to sweat from his almost completely bald head, which reflected the glare from the overhead bulb. He started to rise and said, "I am leaving. Enough with this childish game."

Sitting next to him, Chris forcefully pushed him back down with one hand.

Now standing with both hands on the table, David told him in a calm voice, "Hear me out. If you still want to leave, then do so."

"For your own good, shut up, Gregory, and listen," Tracy said.

Seeing he was outnumbered four to one, he chose to say nothing.

"I am going to make you an offer and you're going to accept," David said.

Now ready to talk, Gregory said, "I am the president of Northwest State Bank here in Great Falls. You can't talk to me that way."

"He just did," Lamar said, reaching for the coffee pot and a cup.

Stroking the stubble on his face, David laid out his plan. "We won't go into all the nasty positions you were in. Suffice it to say there's a price to pay. You're going to launder money from Miss Tracy's enterprise, plus false invoices and receipts."

Now almost shaking, Gregory asked, "Or else what?"

"Or else this DVD of your sordid sexual hang-ups goes to your wife and kids, plus one will go to your boss at your corporate headquarters in Bozeman. We did our homework," David said, grinning at Gregory.

Gregory's temperature was starting to spike as new beads of sweat formed on his heavy face. This time, with all of his strength he had and faster than Chris's hand, he stood and pointed at Tracy. "You bitch! You used me!" he shouted.

Reeling backward in her chair, she responded, "Everybody uses someone in life."

"Sit down, fat boy," David said to Gregory as he looked at Tracy.

For the first time since his doctor advised him to quit smoking, Gregory put his hand to his chest and said, "I'm having chest pain," as he slumped into his chair. "You're insane. I'm going to the police. This is extortion."

Chris reached over and grabbed his silk tie, almost choking him, and said, "That's life. Do you want to see death?"

"Do you want to risk this DVD being shown in court?" Lamar asked, sipping his coffee.

Tracy stood and told Chris, "Stop, you're going to kill him!"

Chris looked at David, who nodded, and he let go of Gregory. David liked the fact that everyone agreed to the plan. He reached into his vest pocket and pulled out 25 hundred-dollar bills. "And to sweeten the deal, here's twenty-five hundred dollars to start," he said as he tossed them at Gregory. They bounced off his belly and fell into his lap.

"Think of the money your bitch of a wife will never see," Tracy said, trying to get him on board. His eyes widened as he looked at the bills.

David asked, "Mrs. Cameron doesn't know of your fun time with Tracy, does she?"

Gregory looked at David, then the money, as he said, "No, and I don't want her to either."

"Good. Do we have a deal?" David asked.

Stuffing the money into his Prada suit chest pocket with fat, sausage-like fingers, he said, "In principle, yes."

The room erupted in laughter. Lamar patted him on the back.

David, feeling like the worst was over, asked, "How's the chest pain now?"

With a smug look on his face, Gregory said, "Money always will be the best medicine," patting the bills through his suit.

"But there's more than just me to think about. There's my assistant bank manager, for one. She's by the book," he added.

"Miss Leann Blake, I believe," David said. "I know who she is. I've made deposits at your bank on Riverside Drive many times," he added. "Never more than five thousand dollars at a time. She handles the transactions," he continued.

"You'll have to space them out over time without drawing attention to yourself with suspicious activity reports—SARs, and currency transaction reports—CTRs," Gregory responded. "How many times in the last month have you made deposits over five thousand dollars?" he asked, leaning towards the table to hear.

"Three in the last month that I can think of," David said, suddenly feeling the long arm of the law.

"Then more than likely a SAR has your name on it," Gregory said. "You've been smurfing. It is a term banks use to show someone suspiciously cashing checks or deposits over five thousand dollars regularly," he said, feeling the pain in his chest returning. "We have to keep those reports on file with corporate in Bozeman. That's where Blake will drive to on Monday. Around eight-thirty she leaves," he continued.

David asked him, "What happens to the reports then?"

"A red flag goes up if too many are filed on the same account. Then the Financial Crimes Enforcement Network and the Financial Intelligence Unit, part of the Internal Revenue Service, make a determination if an investigation is warranted."

"You're the bank president. Can't you take them and make them disappear?" Tracy asked.

"I can take care of the copies at the bank, but Blake takes the originals home on Fridays so she can leave for Bozeman from there, down Interstate 89," Gregory said. He put his hands together behind his head and leaned back in his chair. "It all starts with Blake and those reports. I'll make sure no more SARs and CTRs get filed from now on," he assured everyone.

"How much money we talking about?" Lamar asked David.

"Tracy's going to earn the bulk of it lying on her back. She knows of many rich men out there willing to pay top dollar for her special skills, don't you, babe?"

"Upwards of a thousand to fifteen hundred dollars a night, sweetie," she replied. Glancing at Gregory, she said, "Montana's full of rich bankers and cattlemen willing to pay for that little-girl look, which I can still pull off."

His face turned as red as a Montana beet in the summertime. "I think I've earned the right to tell you to shut up," he said.

David stood and slapped him in the face as hard as he could. "Don't you ever, even in your dreams, tell her to shut up, understand? Or Chris here is going to pound you into the dirt like a tent stake. And another thing: your nights with her are over. Find somebody else to play momma to your fetish, you fat bastard!"

Wiping a trickle of blood off his lips with his handkerchief, he replied, "I got it."

As David regained his composure, he looked into Tracy's eyes as he sat back down. In her brown eyes he felt the love he never had as a child. She knew he loved her and would protect her. He hated the fact that she made her living on her back. They desperately wanted out of Montana. They talked of moving to Dallas and getting married in a few months, once they had enough money. She was the only person he trusted.

"Let's not get ahead of ourselves. Our main concern is those damn reports and how to get them back. Let me think."

"We'll have to make sure Blake never gets to Bozeman with those reports. What kind of car does she drive?" he asked Gregory, with the eyes of a Bengal tiger ready to pounce.

With a feeling of a turn for the worse coming on, he said, "A blue convertible. Why?"

"Let's get one thing straight. I am never going to prison to die like my old man did," David said as he stroked his face once again. "Chris, get off your ass and find me a map of Montana."

Fields reached behind to a side table drawer and found a worn, folded map. He opened it and spread it out on the oak table so everyone could see. David ran his hand over the map and said, "Great Falls to Bozeman, the quickest route is Interstate Highway 89 all the way to Highway 191. Here, before White Sulphur Springs, she will have to drive through Lewis and Clark National Forest. At this sharp bend is our best chance." They all gathered around him like hogs at the trough. "This is where we will ambush and kill her." He pointed to a spot on the map.

Gregory shouted, "Now hold on. Nobody said anything about murder!"

Lamar grabbed the DVD and waved it up to his face. "Maybe you're not with us after all."

"I need time to think. It's hot down here," Gregory said, loosening his tie.

"Not as hot as that DVD," David snorted back. "Besides, you're not the one doing the killing," he said, as he looked at Fields. Turning to Gregory, he said, "You just make sure there's no more SARs and CTRs with my name on them. If you don't want to know any more, leave. But remember, we'll be watching you and your family."

As Gregory stood, David eyed him looking at the DVD in the center of the table. David said to him, "Don't even think about it." Gregory shook his head with disgust as he made his way towards the stairs.

"Enjoy the money and stay in touch through Tracy," David said, glad to see him not put up much of a fight. He turned towards the monitor and watched him exit through the front door out to the parking lot.

Gregory stood next to his Lexus, wiping his head and face with his handkerchief. He looked at the outside of the pawn ship and saw a security camera looking at him and whipped a middle finger before driving away.

"Fat, slow bastard," David said, snapping his fingers at Tracy. "Follow him. See where he goes."

She sprinted towards the stairs as she said, "He's fat, but he ain't stupid. He'll play along. Call me later."

"I'm not going to have the Feds crawling all around here looking for two ex-cons into money laundering and prostitution," David said, walking back to the table.

Turning to Chris and Lamar, he said, "We've got to get those reports back or we'll all be looking at jail time. I can't let Blake live; she'll just file new reports. We have no choice but to kill her. With her gone, that only leaves Cameron. We need him to take care of the copies."

Chris was going to ask a question. David waved him off and said, "Let me think," walking around the table to look at the map. Running his finger over the route she would take, he pointed and said, "Here is where we'll ambush her. Do we still have those *ROAD CLOSED* signs and reflective vests in the shed out back?" he asked without taking his eyes off the map.

"Yeah, that junk is still in there. Why?" Lamar asked.

"I'll need you both to listen carefully to what I'm going to say," David said, rubbing his eyes. "I want you both to drive in the white van to this spot on Highway 89 before the sharp turn. Chris, drop off Lamar and that dirt bike out back with a *ROAD CLOSED* sign and head to a spot just beyond the sharp turn. Wait till Blake slows down and then pull out in front of her and block her in. Lamar, follow when she passes by after putting the *ROAD CLOSED* sign out. There should not be any traffic at that time of the morning. Let's hope Cameron is right, and be in place around eight-fifteen."

He paused to consider his thoughts, then continued, "Make sure to take her cell phone first and then kill her with a knife after getting those reports. Chris, after you do it, take the cycle with Lamar, and I'll meet you both at that twenty-four-hour coffee shop in White Sulphur Springs. Lamar, after she drives by, call me. Then I'll report the van stolen to the pigs. We'll get gas and drive out there this afternoon to look around. After we wipe all the prints off the van, make sure you both wear gloves. Any questions?"

Lamar asked, "Man, there's no other way?" David shook his head no.

"I'll take the bitch out," Chris said, pulling a Bowie knife out of his boot, "in a blink."

"We have to stick together on this. Lamar, get the vests and road signs. Chris, find a couple of pairs of work gloves and rags. Any coffee left?"

3

Like most summer days in Sun Prairie, Montana, John Daniel Urbain awoke with his four-year-old black Labrador licking his face.

"Oh, get off me this morning, Prowler," he said as he pushed him away.

The dog jumped off the bed and made his way towards an old wooden rocking chair in the corner of John's bedroom. The chair was given to John as a gag gift from his employer, Skyway Tours and Transport. Skyway was a helicopter company at Great Falls International Airport.

John hated that chair. It only served to remind him of his age. At 42, he was beginning to show his years.

He loved flying helicopters at Skyway for the past six years and he knew he was good at it. Hauling the out-of-state tourists around Montana was getting old, he had to admit. He ran his hands through his brown hair and asked Prowler, "Where am I going in life?" as the dog yawned and tilted his head with his tongue hanging out. "Ah, to be my own boss someday and spend my Mondays in bed with a good woman," he said. Prowler barked and leaped off the chair, making his way down the hallway of John's home. "I know, you've heard all of this before," he said, disappointed that the dog left.

Deciding to talk to himself, he rolled out of bed and said, in the hope Prowler would hear, "At least grant me a good woman to wake up to instead of your ugly old mug. I need some excitement and maybe a thrill."

Looking over at his alarm clock on the dresser, he read 6:12 A.M. "Damn, I got to get moving," remembering he had to pick up Ryan Porter on his way to work. "I wish he'd buy himself a decent used car," he said as he made his way towards the bathroom for a shower and shave.

✣ ✣ ✣

As he put Prowler in his backyard cage for the day, John said, "It's going to be a beautiful June day today, maybe in the low seventies. Be a good boy and I'll see you later."

Wearing his white Skyway tee-shirt and jeans with brown cowboy boots, he drank the last of his coffee. He walked around the garage to his blue Chevy Silverado. Ryan Porter lived only a few blocks from John's house, so it gave him time to think of his day. His flight with a freelance photographer wasn't till 9 A.M., so he had some time.

Pulling into Ryan's driveway, he could see him and his wife kissing at the front door of their ranch house. *Lucky bastard*, John thought.

Ryan was in his middle thirties, married with three kids; a great helicopter mechanic and a dude John could trust. He always smelled of hydraulic fluid and grease. Today was no exception as he opened the door and climbed in. With some kind of film on his hands, he ran them through his thick black hair and asked, "So, how was your date last night, and more important, was she good in bed?"

As John pulled out, he shook his head and said, "Well, that didn't take long for you to ask. We parted ways after dinner at Ray's Steakhouse," John said, really not wanting to bring it up.

"Why?" Ryan wanted to know. He was always asking questions about John's relationships with women. *Maybe that's all he has left after being married for 18 years*, John thought.

"She's not into flying or helicopters or anything outside of talking about her ex-husband, whom she hates. It went downhill from there," John said.

"You never know, today may be the day you find the right one," Ryan said, trying to put a positive spin on it.

"I'm done with blind dates. It's just not worth it anymore."

"Well, you've always got Skyway to keep yourself busy."

"I need some excitement in my life. I'm growing stagnant without a good woman to be with," John said, feeling sorry he brought it up.

✣ ✣ ✣

Pulling into Skyway's parking lot, John frowned as he caught sight of Annie Webster's green Audi. "I see the bitch is already here. Time to put my game face on. I wish I could find another job. I like flying, but this tourist thing is starting to get me down."

"What do you have against her? She sold you a twenty percent share in Skyway. You're a part owner."

"I guess I want to be my own owner, that's all. It's probably just jealousy."

"See you inside," Ryan said, getting out of the truck.

"I'll be there in a minute," John said, not wanting to work today. He thought of asking Walter Clark to take his flight.

He took a few moments to compose himself and as he went to open the door, he spotted Annie coming out for a cigarette. She was the owner of Skyway and a true workaholic. At 48, she put her heart and soul into the company after her husband died of a heart attack eight years ago. She was left with debts and three helicopters, and she looked haggard from the stress.

As he walked to the hanger office, he said, "Good morning, Annie."

"Yeah, whatever. When are you getting a haircut?" she asked.

"It's on my to-do list."

"Do it fast," she said. "Like today."

Annie put out her butt, waited for John to open the door, and said, "Your six-month FAA exam is coming up. Don't forget."

John opened the door for her and followed her in.

"Oh, I see chivalry isn't dead. Thank you," Annie said. "How was your date last night?" she asked with a coy smirk on her face.

"Was the Hindenburg an aviation disaster?" He rolled his eyes at her.

"Well, you could just give up and accept the fact you may be alone," Annie said.

"Oh, thanks a lot; that really helped," John said.

They both saw Lisa, the young, new, blond secretary. Ann grasped his arm and whispered, "How about her?"

"She's what, early twenties? I'll file that away under not going to happen."

Annie didn't like resistance to her suggestions. "Okay, your photographer called. She's running late. Grab some coffee, put your flight suit on, do your preflight, do something till she gets here."

He made his way to the coffee lounge and saw Ryan with Walter Clark, who had his head in his hands. "Morning troops," he said, pouring himself a cup of coffee.

Ryan looked at him, said, with distaste, "Don't ask," and left the room.

At 54, Walter was on the down side of his career as a pilot. Before John could ask what was wrong, Walter said, "Fucking war. We never should have gone there."

"Which one?"

"All of them," Walter shot back. He was going through Vietnam PTSD, and being a Special Forces pilot back then didn't help his disposition most days.

John could see a little of himself in Walter because of his age. "One day at a time, my friend," John said, trying to ease him out of it.

Coming back to the present, Walter asked, "What's on tap for you today?"

"Just one flight along Highway 89 to Bozeman, then up to Helena, along the eastern edge of the Rockies. Same tour we've all had."

John could see that Walter had more than his itinerary on his mind.

"By the way, any thought on selling your twenty percent share in Skyway to me?"

"I know you were close to Annie's husband, but I am going to hold on to it for a while. I'm sorry."

"You should be. That twenty percent should have been mine."

John was not in the mood to be told off. "Then you should have saved your money instead of blowing it on loose women and booze."

"Up yours, you prima donna," Walter said.

"I don't need this crap. I've got a flight to think about," John said as he walked out.

"What goes around, comes around," Walter said in a loud voice.

John stopped and turned around to ask, "What does that mean?"

"It means your time is gonna come, and I'll be there to see it does."

"Shut up and have another drink, you bastard." John stormed off and headed for the locker room.

After changing into his dark-blue flight suit and putting aside Walter's venom, he walked into the hanger. He caught sight of the only woman in his life—a Bell Jet Ranger 206B, medium blue with black trim, and he loved her.

"Hello, girl. You going to treat me right today?" he said aloud to the craft.

Reaching into the open window to the cockpit for the preflight checklist, he touched her like a gentle woman, softly stroking her contours. Every time he performed a preflight now, it reminded him of his pilot's license exam. He flunked the first time out, having forgotten that step. He thought maybe it was the pot he used in the early days of his Air Force career at Malmstrom AFB down the road. He was a hydraulic specialist back then, but always wanted to learn how to fly. After getting that license years later, he lied to Annie to accept employment at Skyway, and it haunted him. Those days were behind him now, he reasoned with himself.

Lisa broke into the soft music that was playing over the loudspeakers to say, "John to the front office, your ride has arrived."

✣ ✣ ✣

"Hello, glad to meet you. My name is Laura Kennedy," she said, extending her hand. She was older than John had expected—early fifties with brownish-silver hair. He was disappointed as he shook her hand.

"Hello. So what's it like being a freelance photographer?"

"Great. I do a lot of photojournalism for newspapers, *National Geographic* and such. Some war photos too. I've been to Iraq and Afghanistan," she said with a New York accent.

"I can't promise any war photos, but here at Skyway Tours and Transport, we aim to please. This way to the helicopter," John said, extending his arm and bowing slightly.

As they walked to the helicopter, the thought of Ryan saying maybe today John would find a woman popped into his head. He wondered how at 3,000 feet.

4

The trees of the Lewis & Clark National Forest were in full bloom as Lamar Singleton and Chris Fields made their way down Route 89.

"I love the smell of the forest this time of the year," Chris said as he rolled his window all the way down in the white cargo van.

"Man, what does it have to do with the fact you're going to kill this woman!? You never should have brought Tracy into this mess. What if something bad happens?" Chris had called Tracy Burke and asked her if she wanted in on David's plan. She wanted to help.

"What could go wrong? Don't answer that and just do your job," Chris said, irritated at Lamar's sudden change of heart.

"David isn't going to like this," Lamar said, nervously tapping both feet on the floorboards.

"Just relax. What he doesn't know won't hurt him. And besides, he's got enough to worry about." Chris figured they would have to move fast, so he had a loose-fitting black tee-shirt and jeans on with his python boots for possible shit-kicking.

Lamar said, adjusting his bib overalls, "Man, I hate wearing gloves. They make me look stupid."

"You don't want to leave prints in the van, do you? And put on your reflective vest. You're almost there."

"Man, it's going to be hot today," Lamar said. The fog in the low-lying areas was quickly burning away.

Neither of them had ever been involved in murder. Chris made up his mind to take the plunge towards a possible life sentence. Lamar wanted to leave and start pimping in Seattle or Los Angeles if he could break away from the hold Longtree had on him.

"You remember to bring some firepower?" Chris asked.

Reaching behind him, Lamar brought out two guns wrapped in an old rag. "Two Smith & Wesson revolvers, a .38 and a .45 David got off of some local in trade, off the books," Lamar said.

Chris's eyes filled with hate as he thought of the woman he would kill. "I am going to get me some today if she's good-looking. Either way, she's as good as dead."

"Take the damn .45 and shove it where the sun don't shine, you evil fuck," Lamar said.

"When I kill her, what's the difference what I take from her?" Chris said, patting his Bowie knife strapped to his belt. "How we doing on time?" he asked.

"Eight-ten. We're cutting it close."

"Not as close as she's going to get. Just put the sign out after she drives by, then hightail it back to the van and you're done. After I grab this bitch, you and Tracy can head to the coffee shop in her car and wait. It won't take me long. I'll meet you there driving the motorcycle."

Reaching the drop-off point, he pulled over at the south edge of the Lewis & Clark National Forest. "Here's where you get out. Remember to put the sign out after Tracy flashes her lights and they drive by."

Shifting into drive after Lamar removed the sign and motorcycle, Fields could only think of tasting her before he put the knife in.

✣ ✣ ✣

With no oncoming traffic to contend with, Chris put the *ROAD CLOSED* sign at the intersection of Highway 89 and Highway 12. He drove back to an old logging road that was well hidden off the road.

Behind a grove of spruce pine trees, he turned the radio to an oldies rock station up loud. He found The Doors "Riders On The Storm" halfway through. He sang along, grasping the steering wheel as if it was her throat. "I am going to enjoy this. I want her to fight," he said to himself. He spent the time waiting playing with his knife, rolling it over from hand to hand, and getting a hard-on.

✣ ✣ ✣

Tracy pulled over her red Dodge Intrepid and watched her mirror for the blue convertible that was to appear over the hill on Highway 89.

She loved David but this was too much. She thought maybe she could earn more money in Dallas alone without David, but he could not will herself to leave him. She looked at herself in the overhead mirror and was sure of it.

Just then the convertible came into view, cresting over the hill behind her. Tracy pulled out behind it as it drove by. Catching up, she stayed far enough back so as not to scare the woman into thinking she was being followed. *Why am I doing this?* she thought.

✣ ✣ ✣

Leann Blake was thinking she was just glad to get out of the office for a while. She liked making this run to Bozeman every two weeks. At 37, with long black hair, bluish-green eyes, and slender legs, she knew she was a looker without being vain. She knew she had a talent to succeed in banking and maybe be a bank president herself someday if she played her cards right. Today she was thinking only of her future at Northwest State Bank as an assistant bank manager. She made assistant manager status after six years, and she was glad she didn't have to lie on her back to obtain it.

Up ahead she saw a black man in a reflective vest standing next to a motorcycle, holding a sign of some sort. *Why is the person behind me flashing their lights and driving too close?* she wondered.

As she passed the man by the side of the road, she looked in her rearview mirror. He ran to the middle of the road and put the sign out. The car behind her eased up on the gas as they came to a sharp bend in the road.

"Careful, Leann, don't go all paranoid just yet," she said to herself as she slowed down to make the turn.

After they passed by, Lamar ran to the dirt bike and gave it a few kick-starts. It sprang to life and, seeing no traffic in either direction, he pulled out and caught up to the Intrepid.

5

"We're over Lewis and Clark National Forest. We just passed the town of Monarch on your right," John Urbain said into his headset from the left seat to Laura Kennedy, sitting behind him to the right.

"What a beautiful mountain range. What's it called?" she asked.

"The Little Belt Mountains. We're at three thousand feet, so yeah, you get a fantastic view. If you look out of your window on your left, you'll see two golden eagles in a mating freefall." He was glad to have her to talk to. It helped ease the loneliness of not having a girlfriend.

"Got it. That's a keeper photo," she said, adjusting the telephoto lens on her digital Nikon. "Sure beats getting shot at in the Middle East," she joked.

"I bet. Let me know if you want an altitude change. The day is perfect for flying."

"Let's go down to one hundred feet."

"You got it. That's Interstate Highway 89 below. It acts as a canyon cutting through the range," he said as he started descending.

As Urbain was clearing the treetops, a blue convertible in mint condition came into view with the top down. He had seen this car a few times before on this route, but never the face of the black-haired woman driving.

"There's that woman in the convertible again," he said before he remembered he wasn't alone.

"What car, where?" Laura Kennedy said, focusing on the surroundings outside her window.

"Could you get a picture of that convertible with the top down on your left? I'll pay for it," John asked.

Now the day was worth getting out of bed for, John thought, *if the photographer could get a picture of her face and maybe her license plate.*

"The blue one?" Kennedy asked, shifting to a longer telephoto lens.

"That's the one," he said like a boy on his first date, excited but nervous.

"Do you know her? She appears to be a good-looking woman."

"No, just somebody I've seen while flying a few times," he said, trying to catch a glimpse of her.

✣ ✣ ✣

Chris Fields turned to notice the convertible slow down to make the sharp turn south, followed by Burke and Singleton. He gunned the van with his foot on the brake. "It's showtime," he said, tightening his seatbelt.

Turning off the radio, he immediately heard the *whop-whop-whop* of rotor blades slicing the heavy air. "Where the hell did that come from?" he said, pounding the steering wheel. He was straining his neck out of the window for the source of the sound. "The hell with it," he said and punched the gas pedal. He slammed into the convertible broadside, lifting it off the ground on two wheels, with safety glass strung across the highway.

✣ ✣ ✣

"Hey, did you see that? Look out your east window. There's been an accident of some sort. Looks like it was done on purpose. I am going down to investigate. Flight 27 to dispatch, over," Urbain said.

"Go ahead, how's your flight, over," Lisa responded.

"Never mind that. I need the police and an ambulance ASAP, over," Urbain said.

✣ ✣ ✣

"What's that asshole doing?" Tracy said as she narrowly missed slamming into the back of the woman's car.

"I knew it," was all Singleton could say as the bike skidded off the road to the left, ending up on its side.

"Fuck them all," Fields said, unbuckling himself as he kicked the door open that was hanging off its hinges.

Burke ran up to him. "What the fuck did you do that for with a helicopter overhead?" She pointed to the commotion in the sky.

"Shut up, bitch, and get those reports. I'll take care of the helicopter."

She came back with, "Get them yourself," and ducked behind her car.

✣ ✣ ✣

"Laura, you getting all this?" Urbain asked, going into a hover over them.

"I'm on it. I'm already thinking of tomorrow's headlines. Don't let me stop you."

"The police are on their way. Careful, the blond guy's got a gun," he said, pulling the cyclic stick back to give distance.

Pushing the dirt bike off himself, Singleton bit his lower lip to quell the pain coming from his left leg. With a heavy limp, he made his way towards the Jet Ranger and aimed, waving his .38 pistol. "I ain't going back to prison over this shit." He fired four quick rounds.

"There's another gun, get down!" John saw the flashes as his windshield was peppered with rounds forming a spider's web. Two rounds grazed his seat, just missing Laura's head.

"Now it's a war zone!" Laura shouted as she ducked, still taking pictures with her right hand above the seat.

Maneuvering the craft to straight on, John said, "Take this," turning on his dual searchlights in the hope of distracting them with the glare. Even in the daytime, the lights were blinding.

Singleton dropped his gun when the light hit his eyes. "You prick!" he yelled.

Fields took aim and fired a round that found its mark in a support beam to the right of Laura. John lowered and moved the Jet Ranger towards him to swirl gravel and dirt in Fields' face and eyes, knocking him over as he fired a round. The round tore into John's left shoulder blade as blood splattered the cabin.

Losing control momentarily, John hit the throttle and climbed behind a line of pine trees.

Staggering with dirt in his eyes, Fields made his way to Leann's car and was met with a hot cup of coffee to his face. He dropped to his knees and screamed from the burn.

Seeing Fields go down, Tracy stood and made her way to the driver's side door of her Intrepid. She threw herself in and fumbled for her keys. "Oh, please start, please, dammit!" she said, flooding the engine with Singleton running towards her yelling, "Don't leave me here!"

She locked the door as the Intrepid roared to life. She jammed it into reverse and sped off in the opposite direction of the police siren approaching.

Singleton fired a shot at her, shattering the rear window. He limped to Leann's car as she was in and out of consciousness. Reaching in, he grabbed the leather bag containing the reports. He threw the bag at Fields, screaming, "Here's your fucking reports, you sadistic bastard!"

Fields swung the bag over his shoulder.

Now able to see and thinking only of self-preservation, Fields ran to the dirt bike before Singleton could. As he picked up the bike, he pushed Singleton off with all of his strength. "You're on your own, asswipe," he said, kicking up dirt and speeding into the dense woods, leaving him standing there alone.

"Now it's time for you to die, fucker." Taking careful aim, Singleton squeezed the trigger to hear only an empty click. As he reached into his back pocket for some more rounds, he heard, "Drop it or I shoot" from a female highway patrol officer.

"I'm dead already. Take your best shot, pig." He tried to reload and got one round in, walking towards the officer. He yelled, "The hell with it," and aimed.

A round hit Singleton between the eyes and lodged in his brain.

✣ ✣ ✣

"Oh my God, Dave, pick up, pick up!" Tracy said, speeding away at 75 mph, wiping the tears away. "Please, baby!" she screamed into her cell phone.

She heard, "Where's Chris? Why hasn't he called? Where are you?"

"Baby, there was a helicopter, and that asshole Chris…"

She dropped her cell phone as a coyote ran in front of her. Spinning the wheel to avoid hitting it, she lost control, jumped a ditch, and slammed into a large pine tree head-on, forcing her through the windshield.

✣ ✣ ✣

His right cheek was burning as Fields had his hands full maneuvering through the forest. "Fucking bitch," he yelled, trying to form a plan to heap all the blame on Singleton. More than likely he was dead already, he thought. At least he hoped so. That would solve the problem of who had called Burke to ask her to help out. Put all the blame on Singleton, that he was sure of. He had only a vague idea of where he was or how he could find his way back to the pawnshop.

Then there was Longtree to contend with.

As for Burke, the hell with her. Maybe she was dead also.

Where in hell did that helicopter come from? Fields wondered.

6

"I am putting her down next to the highway. You okay back there?" Urbain asked Kennedy.

"I'm a little shaken as such, but I'll live. That was incredible. It looked as if they wanted to kill that woman you wanted a picture of," Kennedy responded.

Bringing the Jet Ranger over the dense treetops for a landing, he saw an officer waving his hands as if to say, *Land here now*.

John worked the collective and cyclic sticks to bring her in slowly. Setting her down, he noticed four squads plus the highway patrol. All of the officers had their guns drawn.

"Easy now, nice and slow," Urbain said, trying not to alarm the officers.

As he shut down the engine and pulled on the rotor brake to slow and stop the blades, a female officer opened the cabin door. "Freeze, don't move. Let's see your hands, both of you!"

Raising their hands, they both climbed out of the helicopter and were forced on the ground and arrested. John Urbain winced in pain as his arms were placed behind his back to be put in cuffs. Laura Kennedy said to the female officer, "Don't cuff me, I feel sick."

The officer said, "If you're going to puke, don't do it in my squad."

"Flight 27, this is Annie, can you hear me?" she said over the two-way radio on the helicopter.

Ignoring her and unable to answer anyway, Urbain tried to scope out the woman's car and catch a glimpse of her as he was thrown in the backseat of a squad. With him in one and Laura Kennedy being led to another, he could only guess at the unknown woman's injuries.

He watched as Laura asked to be un-cuffed again as she felt sick. A female officer shook her head no and was rewarded with Laura vomiting on her boots as John closed his eyes tightly. With her chin, Laura motioned towards the dead man under a gray blanket in an ever-widening pool of blood.

John opened his eyes and said to the sergeant who was writing a report in the front seat, "That's enough to make anyone sick." The sergeant looked over at the body and nodded in agreement.

A sharply dressed man in his fifties, who John guessed was a detective, came walking towards the squad. The sergeant got out and closed the door behind him. They talked and the sergeant nodded, heading to the Jet Ranger.

John could see a gold shield hanging from the man's belt—surely a detective. Opening the door, the detective said, "I'm Detective Dana Lewis. I can remove the cuffs now if you'll stand up." The detective helped John out of the squad, then took the cuffs off.

"Then you know I was at the wrong place at the right time," John said, not happy being cuffed.

"From what the woman in the convertible said, it appears that way. I'd like to get a statement from you. First, what's your full name?"

John answered and asked the name of the woman. Detective Lewis smiled and looked her way. "You mean the looker? Miss Leann Blake, and she's damn grateful you were flying by when you did. Otherwise she'd probably be dead."

"Just trying to help a woman in distress, that's all."

"You're bleeding. I'll get someone to tend to your wound, then we'll talk."

Feeling dizzy, John said, "About time. I thought I was going to bleed to death."

Det. Lewis turned away, yelling, "I need a stretcher here pronto." Turning back to John, he said, "You and Miss Blake are going to take a ride to Great Falls Memorial Hospital for treatment. I'll be there after we sort through this mess."

At that moment, Leann Blake was wheeled past and shouted John's way, making eye contact, "Thanks for helping me. Look me up in the hospital."

In pain but smiling anyway, John shot back, "Count on it, sister," giving her a thumbs-up with his good arm.

A young officer ran up to Det. Lewis and said, "Sir, we have another fatality up the road. Looks like she was fleeing this scene."

Det. Lewis frowned. "Secure the scene. I'll be up there shortly."

"What will happen to the helicopter?" John asked, now lying on a stretcher.

"For now it's going to be impounded as evidence. You're out of Great Falls, right?"

"Yes, Skyway Tours and Transport at the airport," John replied.

"Then that's where we'll take it for now. Let's get you to the hospital. We'll give Miss Kennedy a ride back when I am done with her," Det. Lewis said.

Lying in an ambulance as paramedics worked on his shoulder, John tried not to think of the trouble he was in with Annie. He only knew he had a hospital date with Blake. He smiled through the pain as he thought of what Ryan said about maybe finding his perfect someone today.

✣ ✣ ✣

After composing herself, Laura Kennedy took a deep breath and could still smell the Jet Ranger exhaust. She also smelled a reporter's scoop. Having her camera's memory card taken as evidence, she remembered her cell phone. Casually making her way over to the front of the Jet Ranger, she snapped a few pictures of the damaged craft. Stuffing the phone into her vest, she said to herself, "Now to get the number to the *Great Falls Tribune*, *CNN*, *Fox News*, and *USA Today*."

7

"Tracy, can you hear me!" But the line was dead. Longtree stared at the phone, trying to will a connection.

That was half an hour ago, and she still had not called back. He tried her cell phone, to no avail. *What could have gone wrong?* he thought, giving himself a headache. *What did she mean there was a helicopter? Was it the police? Why was she there with the two idiots?*

Rubbing his forehead to ease the pain that was sure to come, he paced back and forth like a caged tiger. He put the *CLOSED* sign in the front window and pulled the drapes.

Looking at the clock on the wall behind the counter, he saw it was 11:10 A.M. *Why hasn't Fields called from the coffee shop yet? Where in the hell is Singleton?*

For the first time in a long time he felt alone, just him and his open questions to consider. If something had happened to Tracy…no, he would not allow his mind to go there.

Picking up the cell phone off the counter, he decided to call Fields. He hit the speed dial, waited for six rings and said, "Come on, asshole, pick up the damn phone."

Chris picked up. "Hold on till I can shut this bitch down." He was out of breath and could barely talk.

The roar of the dirt bike was disturbing to David's ears. "How come you're on the damn dirt bike? You should be at the coffee house by now. Answer me, dammit!" What sounded like brush and tall grass was all he could hear. He heard the bike throttle up, trying to push higher. Then there was a loud crash as the engine was shut down.

"Yeah, Dave, I'm in a ravine," Chris said, trying to catch his breath.

"Slow down and tell me what happened after you calm yourself," David said, trying to maintain his own control.

"It was all set. The bitch was right on time. Tracy flashed her headlights…"

"Tracy?" David interrupted. "What the hell was she doing there? Where is she?"

"Lamar called her Sunday night and thought we could use an extra hand." He tried to put a positive spin on it. "Anyway, it's over. I got the reports but I wasn't able to take the woman out. There was a helicopter flying over. Me and that dumbass Lamar tried to bring it down by shooting at it…"

David interrupted. "You shot at a helicopter!"

"Yeah, he flew lower and tried to save the bitch in the car. Then I heard the police coming."

"You fucked it all up now!" David said with perspiration forming on his face and rolling down his armpits, trying to comprehend what he was being told. Remembering he still had to call the police to report the van stolen, he said, "Shut up and let me think. Get back here any way you can and hide in the old wood shed. Can you do that, numbnuts? Don't even think of coming in to the shop. Where are Tracy and Lamar now?"

"She took off in her car and Lamar ran into the woods." He knew full well Lamar was probably in police custody, or dead. No telling where Tracy was.

"Just stay in the shed. I'll talk to you later, and you better pray Tracy's okay." He hung up.

David held his head in his hands, trying to formulate a plan on saving his own ass and Tracy's. Taking a deep breath, he called the police to report a stolen van.

✤ ✤ ✤

As he waited for the police, David heard the screech of tires. Looking outside, he saw Gregory Cameron walking to the front door.

"Now what does he want," he said, opening the door before Cameron could knock.

"Mr. Longtree, there's been an accident." Wiping his forehead and looking like death warmed over, he continued, "There's been a fatality on Highway 89. The report was on the news. I was on my way out the door when my wife told me. I saw what looked like Tracy's car slammed against a tree. There had also been some kind of shoot-out down the road from there."

David was stunned and his knees went weak from the news it may be Tracy who was dead. He had to believe it was someone else, he had to. He loved the way she would fawn over him, and now it appeared she was gone.

His first priority was to calm Cameron down from shooting his mouth off. "For now, you just keep your mouth shut till I can sort this out. Nothing changes," David said, looking into Gregory's eyes. "Do you understand me? Don't go to the police or you and your family are dead."

Not forgetting the police were on their way, he reached out and put his hands on Cameron's shoulders to turn him towards the door. "Just stay cool and let me think for a while, and come back in a couple of days."

Gregory said, "I hope you know what you're doing. I've got to get to a meeting in Helena."

"Just remember, keep your mouth shut about our arrangement. Understand?" David added.

Gregory nodded and left, not knowing what to think, or do.

David had an idea that could tie up a loose end. He watched Cameron leave as the police pulled up. He clenched his fists as he thought about the helicopter and Tracy, and the part Chris played in it.

8

As John Urbain was being led into the emergency room, the thoughts came flooding in.

First and foremost in his mind was Miss Blake. Who was this woman, and who were the men trying to hurt her? It did not make sense. He resigned himself to the fact he wouldn't know till he could talk to her, and maybe not even then.

There was no way he was going to just let her get hurt or killed. Was she married? Did she have a family to go home to? Too many questions to fathom. All he knew was he wanted to know her and hoped she was single.

The bright lights of the operating room brought him back to the here and now. How much trouble was he in with Annie? *Will I even have a job to go back to?* he wondered.

Even though his shoulder ached, he knew he did the right thing in helping the woman.

An air tube was fitted over his mouth and someone asked him to count backwards from 100. Then his mind went black.

✤ ✤ ✤

After the x-rays were taken, Leann too had questions with few answers. After it was determined she would spend a few days in the hospital for observation, she cried. The image of her parents popped into her head with her brother and sister. Her head hurt but she was determined to call them as soon as she could.

For now all she could think about was the man who helped her, and sleep.

✣ ✣ ✣

After giving her statement to Detective Lewis, Laura Kennedy was driven back to Skyway Tours and Transport by an officer. Sitting in the back, she could only think of the poor woman and John being shot. But the fact was, her immediate concern was getting the story out for people to read. Taking her notebook and cell phone out, she pushed zero for the operator. "Hello, could you please give me the number for the *Great Falls Tribune* and the number for the story editors for *USA Today, CNN, and Fox News*?"

✣ ✣ ✣

As Detective Dana Lewis was driving up the road to the fatal crash, he wondered if it was related to the incident he just left. Taking a sip of his coffee, now cold, he thought, *Something doesn't feel right. What were they after and what was the significance of the roadblocks?* Something told him there was more to this incident than met the eye. *Who was the dead man in the reflective vest, and who was the one who got away into the woods on a dirt bike?*

9

Having barely slept all night awaiting the return of Fields, Longtree began the day in a foul mood. Waiting for the Tuesday edition of both the *Great Falls Tribune and USA Today*, his thoughts were focused on tying up the loose ends.

The police believed his story about waking up to find the van stolen. He felt confident it could not be traced back to him. Seeing the police always brought back the look on his mother's face when they told her his father would be sent to prison for 10 years. After hearing his older brother Carl's story about their father wasting away in prison, he never wanted to visit there. When he was young, he fled into the woods every time the subject of seeing his father was brought up.

It wasn't long afterward his mother turned to alcohol for comfort and relief till she drank herself to death. He blamed the police for his never having a stable home life. He remembered the midnight rides around Bismarck, South Dakota, with Carl pulling petty crimes and eluding the police. He was determined not to go to prison under any circumstances.

He heard the newspapers being delivered and opened the front door to see the *USA Today* headline: **TWO DEAD IN HELICOPTER SHOOT-OUT IN MONTANA.** This was followed by the *Tribune*'s: **TWO DIE ON HWY 89 AFTER HELICOPTER RESCUE.**

His hands were shaking as he read the names of the fatalities: Tracy Burke and an unknown African-American. The only woman he ever loved, and now she was dead.

He gently laid the papers on the counter. After smoothing the creases with both hands, he attacked the papers and ripped them to shreds.

"Oh, if it's the last thing I ever do, you're going to pay, Fields. You're going to pay," he said to himself.

He felt like throwing something, *but what will that accomplish?* he thought. He gathered up the newspapers and headed to the back door. He was going to build a fire out back and think this through.

Standing at the fire pit, he watched the flames grow, like his hatred. He reached into his wallet and pulled out a picture taken two years ago of him and Tracy at the county fair. He kissed it and started to cry, saying, "I will avenge your death, my sweet," and dropped the picture into the growing flames. "Ashes to ashes."

When the police came to ask about Singleton, he would tell them he must have stolen the van for some unknown reason. Fields would have to lie low till David could formulate a plan on how to use him to clean up the mess he started. Then he would die because of Tracy.

"This John Urbain, Leann Blake, and Cameron are all going to pay, but Chris will pay the most," he said to the flames and crackling wood. "This I swear," he continued.

He fell asleep in an easy chair by the fire as the reddish-pink sun broke over the horizon.

✣ ✣ ✣

Longtree awoke to the distant sound of a dirt bike coming closer through the thick pine tree woods. Looking at his watch while yawning, he read 8:35 A.M.

The sound stopped 50 feet from the tree line. He heard the heavy feet of someone making his way over dead limbs and fallen branches. David reached down, picked up a four-inch knife, and hid it in the back of his pants.

Chris Fields emerged from the wood's edge with grass in his hair, twigs and leaves on his shirt, reeking of sweat, covered with dirt and grime, and boots caked with mud.

David said, with one hand behind his back holding the shaft of the knife, "So, Fields, how's Tracy and Lamar this morning?"

"Fuck you. I rode through the night from the police, eating berries, drinking from a stream, and you want to know about…"

David hit him in the mouth as hard as he could before he could finish. Falling backward, just missing the fire pit, Chris recovered his balance and lunged at David.

"Not so fast, Blondie," David said, pulling the knife out. "If you want to die today, so be it."

Chris reached for his Bowie knife and found only the sheath. "Fuck, it must have fallen out going through that shit," he said.

"What's it going to be then?" David asked, waving the knife in front of him.

Chris reached down for the end of a branch on the fire.

David said, "You reach, you die right here." Chris took a few steps backwards, raising his hands.

David needed him alive for now to tie up those loose ends. He sat down in an easy chair, still holding the knife. "See today's headlines?" David asked.

Reaching inside his torn shirt, Chris pulled out the bank reports. "See tomorrow's headlines!" he retorted, waving them at David.

He said nothing but motioned them towards the fire with his knife. Chris nodded and threw them in. The flames grew higher in the reflection of their eyes.

"Tracy and Lamar are dead," David said, staring at Chris. Chris backed up as David's face turned ashen. "I loved her," David said, wiping his nose on his knife-hand sleeve. "As for Lamar, he was on his way out and was never really happy here anyway. It's still unfortunate," he continued.

"Hey, man, I didn't have anything to do with their deaths," Chris said, raising his arms in defense.

"You fucked it up big time. I put you in charge," David said. "Stay in the shed till we can figure out what to do next. I'll make us some breakfast. The police are still looking for a man with blond hair and will more than likely show up and ask about Lamar. You have to stay out of sight for a while," David said, turning towards the shop.

Thinking only of himself and Tracy, he stopped and asked Chris, "You up for taking that prick Cameron out of the picture?"

"Anything you say, boss," Chris said, heading towards the wood shed.

Walking into the pawnshop, David said to himself, "I'll put dead flowers on your unmarked grave, you asshole. They will all pay for your death, Tracy: Cameron, this pilot Urbain, Blake, and especially Fields," he continued, while making ham and eggs.

"Yes, they will all pay," he said.

10

A thousand miles away in Los Angeles, the sun was rising, sending shafts of fog-ridden beams across the City of Angels. Having never made it back to his cheap motel, Todd "The Mouse" Rudd awoke in his old rusted Lincoln Continental.

There was a tap on the window from a police officer. "Excuse me sir, have you been drinking today?" the officer said with one hand on his revolver.

Rudd was in no mood for a sunrise shakedown. Yawning the fogginess of hangover away, he said, "Last night I did, at that place," pointing to the Last Chance Bar in a rundown section of East LA. "I thought it better to sleep it off than drive."

"Smart thinking. Let's see some identification, please."

As he reached for his wallet, he remembered the Colt .45 revolver under the front seat. As the officer did a background check, Rudd was thinking maybe it was time to make a start in a new city.

He had no place to be today with no job. He lived off his disability check that a shyster lawyer got for him for his bum left leg.

And he had his drugs.

Making runs across the border to Mexico to score cheap weed was getting old.

Rudd played it cool as he stroked his white-and-gray beard. At 44 years old and 5'6", he needed a steady score. Watching his mirror as he combed his brownish-gray hair, he thought again if he would have to use his .45.

"You're free to go, sir. Just try not to sleep in your car in this neighborhood. Have a nice day," the officer said, handing his license back.

As Rudd pulled out, his mouth was dry. He wanted some coffee and something to eat. Turning the corner to a nearby 24-hour restaurant, he wondered if the LA Dodgers won last night, as he had $100 on the game.

Parking the car in the back lot, he walked to the corner to grab the Tuesday edition of *USA Today*. The words "Montana" and "helicopter" caught his eye as he saw the front page.

"What's this about?" he said, thinking it was something about Malmstrom AFB near Great Falls. Having been stationed there, he was interested in all things concerning the base.

As he read the story, he suddenly focused on one name: John Daniel Urbain. "That's got to be him," he said, thinking of the high times they spent together smoking weed off base.

"Now where did I put those pictures of us smoking and getting high?" he said to himself. "If he's such a hotshot pilot now, then he's got money. Looks like I am going to Great Falls, Montana."

Suddenly he wasn't hungry. His mind was on to a possible big score. This time, maybe he could shake down an old friend.

11

John awoke after surgery to a lonely, off-white room on the fifth floor of Great Falls Memorial Hospital. A nurse who assisted with the operation came into his room. "Mr. Urbain? Oh good, you're up. My name is Brenda. Because of what you did for that woman, there's some reporters here for a press conference. Are you up for it? If you are, I'll wheel you down when it's time."

"I'll go. Will she be there?" he asked.

"Yes, she'll be there also."

"I would like to meet and talk to her, if I may, before the press conference."

"She's been asking about you also. Give me a few minutes and I'll take you to her room on the third floor."

✤ ✤ ✤

John was still feeling the effects of the anesthesia as Nurse Brenda took him to the elevator in a wheelchair. He was beginning to feel something he had not felt since he was a teenager. "I am a little nervous about meeting her," he said.

"Don't be. She's looking forward to meeting you," Nurse Brenda said.

"The first time, and I'm in a wheelchair. I'd like to walk, if I can, the rest of the way."

"Hospital rules, I'm afraid," she said, weaving her way through the hallway traffic.

He felt his mouth go dry. "Before I go in, I'd like a cup of water, please."

He pushed the thoughts of the damage to the helicopter out of his mind. More than likely he was going to be in some sort of trouble with Annie because of it.

As the nurse came with the water, he drank it down faster than he wanted. He needed time to think. *What if she's married and I stumble into her room while her husband is there?* he wondered. "Here goes nothing," he said, looking at Nurse Brenda.

"Don't be silly, she's a very nice single lady."

"Wait a minute. She's single?" he said, smiling at the prospect. He adjusted his gown, made sure his hair was straight, and said, "I'm ready now."

She knocked on the door and opened it a little to see if Leann was decent. "Miss Blake, there is someone who would like to meet you. The pilot from the accident is here."

"Oh, please show him in."

Nurse Brenda pushed open the door and said, "Miss Leann Blake, meet Mr. John Urbain. You're a lucky woman because of him."

When they made eye contact, John could see that even in bed with a hospital gown on, she was beautiful. He liked the long black hair that hung past her shoulders. As he came closer, he could see Leann's bluish-green eyes that lit up the room. John thought they were sexy.

"Hello, Mr. Urbain," she said with the biggest smile he had seen in quite some time.

"Very nice to meet you. Call me John." As he reached from the wheelchair to shake her hand, he felt the soft, warm sensation of her touch.

Nurse Brenda said, "I'll leave you two alone. Don't forget about the press conference."

John did not know if it was the sunlight streaming through the window or Leann's touch that was making him warm inside.

Before he could say anything more, a doctor knocked and came into the room. "I am Doctor Jennifer August, Miss Blake. Oh, I see you're with someone. I'll stop back later."

"Anything you have to say to me, you can say to my new friend here," Leann said, pointing to John.

"You have sustained a slight hematoma, which is bleeding on the left side of your brain. Also a concussion with no swelling. I think you'll return to the way you were in due time. You've got a few cuts and scrapes also. I'd like to keep you here a day or two more to make certain there's no more bleeding on your brain. Just try to relax and take it easy. How do you feel?"

"I've got a slight headache and feel dizzy, but due to this man, I'll be fine," Leann said, smiling at John.

"I'm glad I could help," he said, looking into her cat-like eyes.

"Try not to exert yourself too much today. Don't spend too much time at your press conference," Dr. August said. "You must take it easy on your shoulder," she said, pointing to John. "I'll talk to you later after we run some more tests, Leann. Any questions?" Dr. August said, making her way to the door.

"Not right now. Thank you for stopping in," Leann said.

John could not help himself and looked at Leann's right hand for a ring. He did not see one.

Once the doctor was gone, it was Leann who asked him if he was ever married. John said, "No, but I would like to be someday."

"I am glad to hear that," she said. He could see she was about to cry when she said, "You're my hero. Thank you for saving me from those men. I don't understand why they attacked me."

"Remember what the doctor said. Just relax now and let the police do their job," he said, trying to console her. He reached out to hold her hand and felt a shiver run up his spine. He had just met her and already he wanted her desperately.

"I don't really have anyone I can turn to. All my family lives in Casper, Wyoming. I still have to tell them what happened," she said, trying not to cry.

"I'm in the same shape. But one very good thing to count on is each other," he said.

Leann put both her hands out for a hug that turned into a long kiss.

After embracing, they spent the next hour and a half telling their life story to each other.

"I've been an assistant bank manager for a couple of years now. My dream is to open an art studio in Santa Fe, New Mexico, and sell my watercolor paintings to tourists. Sounds boring, huh? Anyway, it's more money than I can afford right now," Leann said.

"I think it sounds great. Can I come too?" he said, joking with her.

"You're welcome to if you can put up with me," she said.

John could smell her hair and perfume and wanted to slide in bed with her.

"I don't even really know you, and I already feel we could make a great team," she said, trying not to cry again.

"Don't cry," he said, stroking her face as he lifted her chin to look into her eyes.

"To think I used to look for your convertible while I was flying. I've always wanted to meet you, but not under these circumstances," he said, trying not to laugh.

"You really did that?" she said as her eyes opened wide.

"Every time I flew, I was hoping to see you driving. You have a unique car. It's not hard to see from the air."

"If you're with me, maybe you could even get me into a helicopter," she said.

"Anytime. And I'll show you how beautiful Montana is from the air."

Nurse Brenda poked her head in to say it was time. "I'll get someone to take you down, Miss Blake, and I'll take Mr. Urbain."

✣ ✣ ✣

John and Leann were both visibly tired after 45 minutes of questions from reporters. Newspapers out of Great Falls and Helena, plus *USA*

Today, showed up to grill them on the rescue. The television stations were there also.

Midway through, Annie Webster and Ryan Porter showed up. She slipped a note to a nurse to give to John. He read it to Leann as his fists tightened at his side. It read that Annie had no choice but to suspend his flying pending a review by the FAA.

"I knew this was coming," he said to her softly. "I know now everything happens for a reason," holding her hand in front of the reporters.

"What will you do if you cannot fly till the investigation is done?" she whispered, looking worried.

"Just have to wait and see," he replied, squeezing her hand in comfort.

12

John awoke Wednesday at the hospital with throbbing pain in his left shoulder. After eating breakfast with two oxycodone 10 mgs for dessert, he felt the pain subside. He turned on the TV, flipping the channels till he found the local news on channel 12, the *Great Falls Today* show.

A slick-haired man in his middle thirties said, "We have more information on the daring helicopter rescue Monday morning on Highway 89, plus footage of yesterday's press conference at Memorial Hospital, coming up."

John could see himself and Leann Blake in the picture in the upper right of the screen as the announcer went on. "The two fatalities have been identified as Tracy Burke and Lamar Singleton. Police Detective Dana Lewis has stated that law enforcement are unsure of a possible motive for the attack. The condition of the woman and the helicopter pilot are said to be improving. The hero, John Daniel Urbain—" John grabbed the remote and turned it off. He did not feel like playing the hero today.

Just then Brenda, the nurse, came in to say he had two visitors. Annie Webster and Ryan Porter walked through the door with dour faces.

"The least you could do is tell me to my face I am suspended instead of passing a note to a nurse," John said, jumping into the fray that was sure to come.

"Good morning," Ryan said, sitting in a chair in the corner.

"Hey, Ryan. Good to see you both," John said, sitting up in bed.

"We had to get back to the shop to assess the damage to the Jet Ranger for the insurance claim. Which, by the way, they're not going to pay because you did not have to get involved. You took it upon yourself to intercede in that mess," Annie said, still standing, which John thought of as a show of superiority over him. "What is the repair going to cost?" she turned to ask Ryan.

He cleared his throat and said, "I'll have to completely check everything, but with the windows, at least one support beam, and a transponder, you're looking at around five thousand dollars to start. Plus the cost of losing the chopper till it's cleared by the police and an investigator from the FAA."

Annie wasted no time getting to the heart of the matter. "You're suspended till the FAA clears you to fly, and I am suspending you till you pay for the damages. What were you thinking with the passenger in back? She could have been killed."

"I'm not sorry I did what I did. And as far as the woman photographer is concerned, she'll probably write a book that will sell for millions," John said as his blood pressure went up.

"Be that as it may, you're still liable for the damages. The choppers belong to me; I own them. They're not your personal playthings," Annie said, stepping closer to John to make sure her point came across.

"I did what I thought was best. I could not just let her die," John responded. "Why don't you just fire me then?" he said, throwing his hands in the air. He knew she was right; he did it more for effect.

"You're too good of a pilot, and it would be bad publicity under the circumstances—firing a hero," she said, trying to bring a little levity to the situation.

The point being made, John had to agree. "I'll pay for the damages somehow," he said, dejected, like a dog with its tail between its legs.

"Good. Then if that's all, I've got to get back to the shop. Ryan, let's go," Annie said, heading for the door. She stopped and turned to face John. "I'm sorry you got shot."

After Annie left, Ryan walked over to John's bed and said, "Don't worry about it. You did the right thing. It took guts."

Shaking Ryan's hand, John pulled him closer and said, "The woman is beautiful."

Ryan laughed and said, "You both looked good at the press gathering."

"Ryan, are you coming or what!?" Annie said from the hallway.

"Take it easy, dude," Ryan said to John as he hurried to the door.

"Any way I can," John said, smiling.

He had only one choice to get the money, and that he did not want to do: Sell his 20 percent ownership to Walter Clark to pay for the damages. He suddenly knew his days at Skyway were drawing to a close.

Nurse Brenda came in to say he and Leann would be going home today. Before he could leave, he made a promise to himself to stop in her room and get her phone number and address. Now that he found her, he was not about to let her slip between his fingers.

13

Detective Dana Lewis sat at his desk at the Great Falls police station and pondered his next move. In his office with the door closed, he laid out all of his paperwork in front of him. In his 19 years on the force, he thought he'd seen it all. This case was different.

He ran his fingers through his black hair, trying to come to grips with the prospect of where to start. At 48 years old, he had the respect of his fellow officers and wanted desperately to solve this case and maybe retire.

He arched his 6' frame as he sat back and drank his coffee. The motive was in front of him, he was sure of it. He just had to find it among the reports and photographs.

On the left-hand corner of his desk was the file on Lamar Singleton, an ex-con from Seattle. What was he doing in a reflective vest and carrying a gun? What was his motive for shooting at an officer?

Next to that was the background and pictures of Tracy Burke, along with a small black phone book of first names, with dollar signs next to the names. Also there were notes on preferred sexual positions. He picked up some of the photos taken by the photographer in the helicopter. Tracy was a good-looking woman. What was her story? The last number she called, according to her phone records, was to a pawnshop in Ulm. "She's a prostitute, I bet," he murmured.

He pulled out a blank white sheet of paper and in the middle of it wrote her name and circled it. In the upper left corner he wrote Lamar's name and did the same.

There were no fingerprints found in the van or on the road signs to give any indication of who the blond-haired man who had disappeared into the woods was. He found a photo of the man pointing a gun at the helicopter, but it was grainy at best. He put the words "unknown blond" in the upper right-hand corner of his sheet and circled it.

Next he looked at the stolen vehicle report. The white van was owned by David Longtree. Looking it over, the address caught his eye: a pawnshop in Ulm. He leaned back and wondered why Burke's last call was to the same number given on the report. On the lower left he put the name David Longtree and circled it. Next he drew a line from Longtree's name to Tracy Burke. He smiled at the connection made.

He leafed through the paperwork to find Miss Blake's report, but saw nothing of significance except the fact that she was an assistant bank manager at Northwest State Bank, heading to Bozeman. He leaned forward and thought maybe it was money they were after. Why did Singleton take the brown leather bag and not her purse that was lying in plain sight? He had to find out what kind of reports were in the leather bag.

He picked up the phone and dialed Great Falls Memorial and asked for Blake's room. After answering on the second ring, he said, "Miss Blake, this is Detective Lewis of the Great Falls Police Department. What can you tell me about what was in the brown leather bag that was taken from you?"

After a ten-minute discussion on CTRs and SARs, he asked if she remembered the names on the account. "No, I am sorry, I don't," she replied.

"No matter. I'll check with the bank. Thank you for your time," he said.

After hanging up, he wrote on his sheet *SARs and CTRs* and circled it in red.

He stood up and grabbed his gray sports jacket off the back of his chair. As he headed out of his office, he wrote on the chalkboard that the department used for the whereabouts of its detectives under his name. In big capital letters he wrote NORTHWEST STATE BANK, RIVERSIDE AVE. Then, underneath it, Longtree Pawnshop in Ulm.

For the first time since he got the call about the ambush, he felt like he was on to something.

14

Gregory Cameron looked at his Rolex watch. It showed 10:38 A.M. He felt relieved. He had come in before everybody else at Northwest State Bank on Riverside Avenue in Great Falls. When he arrived at the bank at 8 A.M., he went straight to the file cabinet to gather all the copies of CTRs and SARs with Longtree's name and account number on them. He found three reports and wasted no time in taking them to his private office. After locking the door behind him, he shredded them. With beads of sweat running down his face and with hands shaking, he knew he had committed a crime. With the thought of Tracy's death still playing in his mind, he felt partly responsible. He picked up a priceless vase from a credenza in his office and threw it against the door.

Next came the inevitable knock on the door. "Mr. Cameron, are you okay in there?" he heard through the door from one of the female tellers.

"Yes, everything is fine. I dropped a vase, that's all," he said, not sure if she believed it.

He felt better now, knowing those reports were gone, but he had to pray that Leann's originals were shredded or burned. He walked over to his phone to call Longtree to see what happened to those reports.

Just then there was another knock on the door. "I said everything's okay. Please don't disturb me," he said.

"Mr. Cameron, there's a detective here to talk to you about Leann Blake's accident," he heard.

He almost tripped over his leather chair getting around his desk to unlock the door. "One minute, please," he said, in a tone that conveyed a trapped animal. Wiping the sweat from his face and hands, he took a quick look into a side mirror to straighten his silk tie. He felt sick to his stomach as he unlocked the door.

"Mr. Cameron, I am Detective Dana Lewis of the Great Falls Police Department. Can we talk about the SARs and CTRs under investigation?" He noticed the broken china strewn throughout the office. "Did I come at a bad time?" Lewis asked with a stern look on his face.

"No, no, not at all. Come in, please. Sorry about the mess. I dropped a vase," Cameron said, starting to think of jail time and wearing a prison uniform. Wiping bits and pieces of the vase from a leather chair, Cameron said, "Please, have a seat."

Feeling a chance to put some pressure on him, Lewis said, "Looks like you did more than just drop it."

Cameron had an image of his father catching him with his hand in the cookie jar and he shivered with fear. "I haven't been feeling well lately," Cameron lied. "How can I help you?"

"Miss Blake was carrying those reports to your corporate office in Bozeman, yes?" Lewis said. "I would like to see the originals, if I may," he went on, hoping to put more pressure on Cameron if he was involved. Tracy Burke's little phone book had the name "Gregory" in it, and Lewis had a hunch in his gut.

"Let me get them for you. If you'll excuse me for a moment," Cameron said as he stood, making his way towards the door.

Lewis made a slow sweeping motion with his right hand to say go ahead. Cameron flashed a smile that Lewis had seen a thousand times on criminals sure they had put one over on him.

As Cameron left the room, Lewis looked at the eight by ten pictures of the little missus on his desk. Her face projected an image of "anywhere but here." Could it be Cameron was in a loveless marriage and that's why he sought the company of a prostitute? Lewis felt a jab in his buttocks from a missed piece of vase as he moved in his chair. He reached to grab it and flung it across the desk in disgust.

As he was about to check his watch, Cameron came in and said, "Here you go. Anything in particular you're looking for?" he asked. Cameron handed him the file, which seemed a little light on weight.

"How many files are in here?" he asked as Cameron sat back down at his desk.

"I'm not sure on how many," Cameron said, feeling like his world was being destroyed slowly.

As Lewis looked over the names on the reports, he noticed they were all over a month old. He looked at Cameron and asked, "These aren't up to date. I thought Miss Blake went to Bozeman every two weeks."

"She does," Cameron said, loosening his tie to breathe. "Those are the most current ones we have, I'm sorry to say."

"I'd like to take these and look them over," Lewis said, lifting himself from the chair.

"I am sorry. Under federal guidelines, the copies must stay here in case of an audit," Cameron said, now standing with both hands on his desk.

"Then I need a federal warrant as well. Good day, Mr. Cameron," Lewis said as he handed the file back to him.

As he was about to exit, he turned and asked Cameron, "Oh, by the way, do you use prostitutes?" feeling like John Wayne at a quick-draw contest.

Stunned at the question, Cameron shot back, "No. Why do you ask?" as he stepped back from his desk with a look of fear. *He knows about Tracy*, he thought.

Lewis smiled and said, "No reason."

As he made his way across the lobby, he broke out in a wide smile and shook his right fist tightly. *I think he's the one*, he said to himself as he went through the door out to the parking lot.

✣ ✣ ✣

As Det. Dana Lewis pulled into the Longtree parking lot, he was sure of two things. First, Tracy was a prostitute. Second, Gregory was a customer. Now to find out why Burke called the pawnshop and what role Lamar Singleton played in stealing the van.

Before he went in, he sat in his unmarked police car and looked at the stolen van report. He looked up and noticed that the drapes had moved at the picture window to the pawnshop. Somebody was looking to see who it was that pulled up.

✣ ✣ ✣

"Chris, stay down in the basement. An unmarked police car just pulled up!" David Longtree said from the top of the stairs. "I told you they'd be back to ask about Singleton," he added.

There was a knock at the door. "Time to let the pigs in," he said.

As he unlocked the front door, he was met with, "Hello, I am Detective Lewis. I'd like to talk to the owner of this establishment," as he flashed his gold badge.

David stepped aside to let him in without saying a word. Lewis could see from the expression on his face he was not wanted here. "Are you the owner?" he asked as he stepped inside the unlit foyer.

"Yeah, I am the owner. What do you want?" David said as he stepped in front of Lewis, blocking further entrance.

Lewis looked around at the cheap knickknacks that were displayed on the counter and shelves throughout. "Nice place you have here," he lied. Just another dive on the outskirts of town. It looked like a playhouse for hoboes and bums. He looked at Longtree, who was dressed in jeans and a torn, dirty, white t-shirt, and thought he had met the head bum.

"Did you know Lamar Singleton and Tracy Burke?" he asked.

"Yeah, Lamar was an employee here for two or three years. But who is this Tracy Burke woman?" David said, clutching his fists as his eyes started to moisten at the thought of her and the plans they had for the future.

Lewis picked up on his body language and said, "She was the woman killed on Highway 89 Monday morning, and her last call was to here."

"Yeah, I remember, I got a wrong number call about mid-morning that day. I don't know who it was, only it was a woman on the other end," David said, standing firm and looking him in the eyes.

"May I come in and have a seat?" Dana asked.

"Why? I told you all I know. It's unfortunate about the girl, and as far as Lamar, I have no idea why he stole the van that day."

"Anybody else work here?"

"No, just me and Lamar," David said, knowing Chris was listening, probably at the top of the stairs.

"How did you and Singleton meet?" Lewis asked.

"He wandered in one day looking for a job, and I hired him," David said.

"That's all I have for now. Thank you," Lewis said, turning to leave. He was not going to get anything more out of Longtree.

He would have to get a court order to review the Northwest State Bank's records. Lewis had a feeling Longtree had known Burke. He would be sure to get hold of his and her phone records, but how to convince a judge it was warranted? *Maybe he's laundering money and Burke is involved*, he surmised.

15

After Detective Lewis left, Longtree wondered if Cameron had destroyed those reports. "He's gone. You can come up now," David said, still feeling the loss of Tracy's death. He could not even go to her funeral for fear of being seen by the police, who were sure to watch for who showed up.

"I was at the top of the stairs and heard everything the pig said. I wouldn't worry about it. They were bound to ask about Lamar. And Tracy, they must have looked at her cell phone to see who she called," Chris said.

"No shit, you figured that out, huh? Well, good for you. Now tell me, what am I supposed to do with you when the whole state is looking for you, with that burn on your face?"

Chris instinctively ran his hand over the burn on his left cheek. "Man, I should have killed her," he said.

"But you didn't, and she can identify you, you stupid bastard," David said, feeling like taking him out back and killing him right then and there. "You're to stay inside the shop, out of sight, and don't answer the door or the phone. You got it?" David said, knowing Chris was a huge liability to him.

David was thinking how to lure Cameron to the shop, where Chris could prove useful in taking him out. First he needed to make sure of those reports. Otherwise, that detective would be back. "Go take a shower and change into clean clothes. I can smell you from here," David said, sick of the sight of him.

Chris was nibbling on some toast and said, "You got anything else?"

"I'll have to use an outside phone and get Cameron over here, and then you're going to kill him. We can't have him free to shoot his mouth off, can we?"

"No, he's just a liability," Chris said.

And so are you, David thought.

✣ ✣ ✣

As Longtree stepped out of the pawnshop, he heard the thunderclap of a summer storm approaching from the west. His blue jeans and shirt were accumulating rain droplets faster than he was able to think. With Tracy's death, his whole plan of money-laundering and living the high life was washed away like rain to a sewer drain.

He opened the door to his Ford Explorer and slid in. Starting the vehicle and turning on the wipers, he pondered the days ahead. First to take out Cameron and dispose of that slob in some hole in the woods. With the motor running and his hands on the steering wheel, he sat and tried to think everything through. He watched the wipers shift from left to right, right to left, and back again in perfect unison. *That's what I need, perfect unison of thought, like seeing a chess move and knowing your opponent's weakness.*

As he pulled out of the lot and turned into traffic, his mind was contemplating the death of Cameron and Fields, closing the pawnshop, and just saving his own ass in another town out of state or in Canada. But someone had to pay for Tracy's death. Someone had to be blamed. Chris would get his in due time. The pilot and Blake were on his list of those to take a hard fall.

First things first: Cameron.

✣ ✣ ✣

Driving around the city of Ulm looking for a pay phone was not how David wanted to spend his afternoon. Seeing a phone up ahead, he pulled up next to it as the rain came down in sheets. He looked through his wallet for the number Tracy had given him, punched the numbers and waited. Cameron answered on the first ring.

"This is Longtree. Did you destroy those reports?" he asked.

"Oh, Mr. Longtree. Yes, I shredded them. But the…"

"I don't want to hear it," David interrupted. "Just take a taxi to the pawnshop tonight around five P.M., and don't tell anyone, get it? We need to talk."

"I'll be there, but the..."

David slammed the phone down. "Now to get Fields on board," he said as he turned around to head back to the pawnshop as the rain subsided.

✣ ✣ ✣

"After I am certain he took care of the reports, I'll want you to take him out of the picture permanently," Longtree told Fields. "We'll get him outside, and after you put a wire around his neck, we'll bury him behind the shed with the backhoe."

"That's the least I can do, considering everything that's gone wrong," Fields said as he brushed cookie crumbs off his t-shirt.

"When I ask him if he likes hunting, that's when I want you to take him, okay?" Longtree asked.

"You got it, boss," Fields said with a smile. He was looking to kill someone to please Longtree.

"After it's done, we'll go to the cabin for some trout fishing and relax," Longtree said, knowing full well he was lying—there would be a vacation, but that would only be for himself.

One kill at a time…one kill at a time.

✣ ✣ ✣

David opened the storefront's drapes, took a folding chair, and rested his feet on the windowsill. It was almost 5 P.M. and Cameron should arrive any minute.

Everything was in place for a killing tonight. Fields took the initiative to have the hole already dug behind the shed.

Looking at the cars that passed by, David smiled to himself for the first time since the ambush. Fields was in the shed waiting for the show to begin. Cameron was on his way to his own death. The pilot and Blake would get theirs in due time. Yes, David Samuel Longtree could see the light at the end of the tunnel.

Longtree had to laugh when he thought of Fields digging the four-foot-deep hole.

A Great Falls taxi pulled up into the lot, and David got up and waited for the knock on the door. "At least he's on time," David said to himself.

After the taxicab pulled away, David answered the door. "Come on in. You want a drink?" he asked Cameron.

Dressed in his Prada suit and tie, Cameron stepped in and said, "I'll take a brandy, neat."

As David made his way to the kitchen for the brandy, he said, "Let's go out back and get relaxed." Cameron walked by David to the back door and stepped outside.

Longtree found a clean glass, poured a drink, and made his way to the backyard. After motioning to a lawn chair by the fire pit, he handed Cameron his glass.

"Does anyone know you're here?" David asked.

"No, I did as you told me—tell no one. The police came to the bank and asked about the reports and Tracy."

"Just like they're supposed to," David said.

"What are we going to do about Blake and that pilot?" Cameron said, shaking as he took a drink of the cheap brandy.

"What can you tell me about Blake?" David asked.

"I know she's afraid of bees. She has to carry an epinephrine pen with her at all times. If she gets stung without it, she's a goner, pretty fast."

"That's good to know. I'll check the Internet," David said, now beginning to sweat. As he wiped his forehead with his handkerchief from his back pocket, he could see Fields opening the door to the wood shed, slowly and silently stepping out.

Focusing back on Cameron, he asked, "You're sure all the originals and copies of the reports are taken care of?"

"Oh yes, there's no record at the bank concerning SARs and CTRs. I made sure of it."

As he was talking, Fields snuck up behind him and pulled out a strand of thin steel wire from his pocket.

"Did your man take care of the copies?" Cameron asked David.

"All taken care of," David said, pointing to the fire pit. He asked Cameron, "Do you like to hunt?"

As quick as a rattlesnake, Fields put the wire around Cameron's neck and pulled him backward in an instant with one leg in his back. Cameron tried with his fat fingers to get the wire off. He waved his arms as his face went reddish-purple and his eyes bugged out.

David stepped back and said, "I told you there was a price to pay." Fields laughed at that and pulled tighter.

Slowly Cameron went limp and fell over as Fields let the wire go. Instinct told him to go for the Rolex watch and the wallet. There was $212.

"Take his wallet and anything else that may identify him. We'll shred his license and credit cards up. Roll the fat bastard over and throw him in the hole," David said.

Fields dragged him over to be dumped. With an effort, he rolled Cameron into the grave and said to David, "That's over with. Time to take a vacation and start over."

"Not yet. Next we take that bitch Blake out," David said with a grin.

"Cover that fat bastard right now," he said to Chris as he downed his glass of brandy.

"I think his jacket will fit me," Chris said. "I'm going to take it."

"Just cover him!" David said, fed up with having to deal with him acting like a five-year-old in a toy store.

16

Having only slept at cheap motels or rest stops for the past two days, Todd Rudd was tired. He was on Interstate 15, thirty miles outside of the city limits of Great Falls. He could tell by the temperature gauge he wasn't going to make it. Even with the defroster and heater going full blast, his Lincoln Continental was overheating fast. He spit out the window at the prospect of having to hitchhike into the city.

The temperature outside was in the low sixties with clouds moving in from the west. Checking his watch, it was Thursday, 10:10 A.M., and the traffic was picking up with the summer tourists. His mind drifted back to his days at Malmstrom AFB and the weekends he spent looking for footloose girls, drinking in cowboy bars, and smoking pot.

Everything he owned was in two suitcases and three paper bags in the trunk. He had cleaned out his bank account of $12,000 in cash and money orders, plus his Colt .45 was under the front seat.

"Well, Sara, I think the time has come to part company," he said to the car as the temperature gauge was pushing its limits. Why he called his car Sara, he could not remember. Maybe it was because of his father's Southern Baptist upbringing and being a hardcore preacher.

"Focus, dammit," he said, trying to bring his thoughts back to the real world. The sign up ahead read *Rest Stop 4 Miles.* With a little luck he would make it and could use a pay phone to call for a taxi.

He loved Montana with its landscape and rolling buttes and he said, "It's good to be back. I'll get some payoff money from Urbain, buy another car or van, and make Great Falls my new home." He could not resist the urge to laugh at his good fortune of the story of John Urbain in the *Los Angeles Times* and *USA Today*. He was confident Urbain would pay a price to keep his good name from being tarnished in the newspapers.

✤ ✤ ✤

"Well, if it isn't the hero Urbain out of the hospital, sniffing around his old stomping grounds at Skyway," Annie Webster said sarcastically upon seeing him enter the building.

"That hurts more than the pain in my shoulder," he shot back, surprised at the tone of her voice.

"Shouldn't you be home? Or have you come to pay for the repairs on the Jet Ranger?" she said, pulling the chair from behind Lisa's desk, who was out to lunch.

"Don't worry, princess, you'll get your damn money. I haven't even been home yet," he said, louder than he expected.

"I don't have time for this now. I've got to get to an appointment with our insurance company because of you," she said, getting up from the chair and walking towards the front door. She stopped in front of him and smoothed the wrinkles of her dark-blue pants suit. Pointing a finger at him with a face of pure anger, she said, "If you ever call me that again, you're fired. Now if you'll excuse me and step aside, I've got to get going. Make yourself useful and answer the phones till Lisa gets back. Can you handle that?" she asked, not waiting for an answer. "Try not to burn the place down," she said as the door closed behind her.

He had to smile and admire the way she handled herself and not be pushed around. "You're one tough lady," he said, taking the chair at Lisa's desk. He threw up his hands and said, "Now we wait for Lisa to get back." He knew now he should have just taken the taxi from the hospital straight home.

✣ ✣ ✣

Annie felt better and smiled as she made her way across the parking lot. *It needed to be said*, she told herself.

Reaching for the car door handle, she noticed a taxicab pull into the lot. A haggard man who looked to be in his late forties got out. Looking like he had slept in his clothes for a few nights, he paid the driver and stroked his gray facial hair with his free hand. He smiled at Annie, who could see his brown teeth from 20 feet away and was repulsed at the sight of him. She watched him for a moment, then said to herself, *Probably just another down-and-out war vet looking for a job or a handout.* She got in her car and drove off.

✣ ✣ ✣

John thought of Ryan Porter working in the hangar and got up from his chair; the hell with answering the phones. The front glass doors opened and he almost fell over at the sight of Todd Rudd.

"And we meet again. How you doing, Urbain? You don't remember me, do you?" he asked, extending his hand towards John.

"How could I forget Airman Rudd? You look terrible." Not wanting to shake hands, he continued, "Now the million-dollar question: Why are you here? I don't do that stuff anymore," referring to the pot they once shared.

Todd snorted. "Even the great John Urbain isn't worth a million. More like ten thousand in cash."

John tilted his head slightly and asked, "What does that mean?"

Todd moved within a foot of John and said, "I'll bet you didn't tell your employer about your pothead days at Malmstrom AFB, did you now? I happened to catch your daring rescue of that woman in the *Los Angeles Times* back in LA. I thought to myself how it would look to your adoring fans if they knew about your sordid past, complete with pictures."

John felt sick to his stomach at the thought of this prick shaking him down.

"I'll expect ten thousand cash, or certain pictures of us smoking weed off base in our uniforms back in the day go to the press, local and national," Todd said.

Now it was Urbain's turn to step closer and say in a loud voice, sticking his finger in Rudd's chest, "Do the slime you hang around with still call you by your nickname? What was it now…The Mouse? I see you graduated to just a rat prick. Where do you figure I'll get my hands on that kind of money?" Bile was forming in his throat at what Leann Blake's reaction to the news would do to their budding relationship.

As Rudd sat on top of a side desk in the corner, he said, "What do I care as long as you get it? I get the money, you get the pictures and the negatives of the past I'm sure you would rather keep hidden."

Having made his point, he stood and walked towards the door. He pulled at his dirty t-shirt and wiped his stained, oily hands on his faded blue jeans. "I'm staying at the Highridge Motel. You remember the nights we spent there in the Air Force with girls, don't you?"

"I know where it is," John said like a beaten dog in front of its master.

"Room 22, hotshot. Be there at five P.M. with the cash," Rudd said.

Just then Lisa came in from lunch. "Oh, John, good to see you. How you doing?"

"Could you please excuse us for a moment?" John said, not wanting her to see or hear what he was going to do.

Lisa looked at Rudd and he smiled at her. Again those brown teeth were not his strong point. "Sure thing. I'll step outside for a smoke," she said, trying to stay as far away as she could from Rudd.

"You're cute," Rudd said, following her with his eyes.

"You're not," she said, trying not to look at him.

As he admired her ass as the door closed behind her, John made his move. He forcibly grabbed Rudd by the back of his neck and with his other hand, took hold of his belt and threw him against a file cabinet across the room. Rudd hit his head against the wall and ended up in a heap in the corner. John moved in, throwing a folding chair out of his way in the process. He seized Rudd by the neck to line up his shot. Rudd could only blink at the sight of John's fist slamming into his jawbone. Trying to shield his face from further blows, he saw stars in front of his eyes. He spit at John and missed, as blood was coming from his mouth. John grimaced as several stitches in his shoulder broke open.

Rudd tried to crawl to the door as John gave a solid kick to his ass as a final act of justice. "Get out and don't show your fucking face around here anymore," John said.

Rudd said, with a mouth full of blood, "You're going to regret this, asshole!"

"Go pound sand," John said with a smile.

What did he care if people knew he once did drugs? Most people experimented at one time or another in their lives. What did concern him was what Leann would think of it. He had just met her and did not want to lose her. He was tired of being alone. If there was to be trust between them, he realized he had to tell her the truth about his past.

Climbing into his Silverado, he sat there and stared at the Skyway Tours and Transport sign that was over the entrance. There was no escaping the fact that his days employed there were probably over because of Monday's incident. He thought of selling his shares to Walter Clark and moving to New Mexico, hopefully with Leann. He closed his eyes tightly and shook his head. He was getting ahead of himself.

Still, it felt good to throw Rudd across the room. A memory of them standing by Union tombstones in Little Bighorn in southeastern Montana haunted him: smoking pot and dancing on graves like they were Sioux and Cheyenne warriors. *That has to be the pictures Rudd was referring to*, he thought.

He was about to start the engine when his cell phone rang. "Hello, this is John," he said.

"This is Leann. I thought of you a lot today and would like to make you dinner tomorrow night. How about coming over around seven-thirty? Then we can talk."

"Babe, that would be great. There's something I want to tell you," John said, happy that she called.

"My address is 3218 View Road in Black Eagle. Do you know where that is?"

"Yes."

"John, I think I am falling in love with you. Does that shock you?"

"No, I feel the same way." He could tell she was about to cry.

"I'll see you at seven-thirty tomorrow, then."

"You can count on it."

At that moment he forgot everything but her.

17

David Longtree did not have a choice. He had to reopen the pawnshop. Deprived of money from Tracy's nightly excursions, he had to have income.

After ordering Chris Fields to spend the day cleaning and dusting off items, the shop was ready. At 9 A.M. on Friday morning, he put the *OPEN* sign in the window and waited. "I hate this," David whispered to himself, unlocking the front door.

He had spent considerable time and effort buying items from flea markets and rummage sales across the state. With Tracy in tow, they would make a weekend of it, traveling around Montana. They bought only the best, stopping to make love in the wild if the mood came over them. Those days were gone now forever, thanks in part to Chris Fields.

"Look at you. Go put on a clean shirt, will you?" he said to Chris as he entered the kitchen.

"That bastard pilot," David said, kicking a trash receptacle across the room. "Someday I'm going to find a way to even the score," he said to Chris, who was busy enjoying his cornflakes. "Is that all you do is eat?" David said, sick of feeding him.

David shuffled over to the coffeepot, which had only half a cup left. "You had to drink the last of the coffee without brewing another, you prick? Make some now," he said over his shoulder as he walked out of the room.

As he pulled the front curtain back, he noticed an old, out-of-state station wagon pulling into the lot. He watched as a middle-aged couple got out, with two children under twelve following behind. "Little brats, picking their noses and eating ice cream to boot," he said to Chris, who had left the kitchen to stand next to him. "I hate kids," David said to Chris, who nodded.

"Me too."

✤ ✤ ✤

After shopping around Great Falls for a gift for Urbain, Leann glanced at her watch: 10:05. "Plenty of time," she said, thinking more of tonight's date with John. Feeling nervous, she felt she had to get something for him to show her appreciation. Not finding anything that piqued her interest, she was about to give up. Then it hit: Try the pawnshop route. Something that said thank you in a special way, but also said it was fine if they ended up in bed together.

With her dark hair in a ponytail and wearing sunglasses, she was getting long looks from men. She also was wearing a black t-shirt, tight-fitting dress jeans, and blue cowgirl boots. Leann smiled at the thought of how she looked to men without being conceited. "Stay calm tonight and just be yourself," she said, making her way through crosstown traffic.

She had a secret to share with John, unsure of how he would respond. She bit her lower lip at the thought of him walking out of her life. She gunned her rental Honda Accord onto Interstate 15, looking for pawnshops, feeling maybe this was all wrong. What did she really know about him? *Maybe he's married and lied to me.* She tried to push that thought out of her head. If only she could find a man who would hang around for the long haul.

Looking to the west at approaching storm clouds that loomed over the Rocky Mountains, she felt uneasy about tonight. She had to hit the brakes more than she would have liked as a car cut her off. She yelled out the window, "Nice move, jackass." *No, don't let it ruin your day*, she told herself.

Up ahead an old, faded sign read *Longtree Pawnshop Next Exit*. Unsure of what she was looking for, she decided to try it out. Pulling into the lot, she had her doubts. The rundown shop gave an air of having not been painted or fixed up in quite some time.

✤ ✤ ✤

The middle-aged couple had left without buying anything, which left Longtree in a foul mood. To add insult to injury, one of the little bastards dropped his double-chocolate ice cream on the freshly cleaned carpet. Having seen the expression of disgust on David's face, the couple thought it best to leave. "And don't come back," he said as they drove away.

He was about to take it out on Chris when the cowbell above the door clanged. As David turned the corner out of the kitchen, he saw her.

"Hello," Leann said as she took off her sunglasses.

"What can I do for you?" David said, admiring her beauty. *Now that's more like it*, he thought.

"Oh, I am just looking," she said, sure that someone was watching her from the room behind the counter.

"Take your time. If I can be of any help, let me know," he said, taking a seat on the chair behind the counter.

Leann strolled around the three aisles, looking at tourist bric-a-brac.

From the kitchen, Chris Fields was eyeing her through a small hole in the wall that was intended to catch shoplifters in the act. Once he laid his eyes on her, he could not believe what he was seeing. There stood the bitch who threw hot coffee on him—Leann Blake!

Shaking his head to clear out the cobwebs, he peered closer to the eyehole. "I want her bad," he said to himself, feeling a tingle in his crotch. He had to get David's attention without drawing it to himself. He sure could not walk out there and introduce himself, as all of Montana was out looking for him.

As he checked out Leann's ass, he noticed David's cell phone on the counter and decided to call. From his cell, he punched in the numbers and smiled at their good fortune of Blake's appearing in Longtree's lair.

Hearing the ring, David frowned and reached over and answered. "This is Chris. Come into the kitchen right now!"

"What do you want?" David said, not in the mood for games.

"It's her, the woman from the ambush, right in your store."

David looked up at Blake, who was meandering her way through the shop, unaware. "Are you sure?" he said, not taking his eyes off her.

"Positive, that's the bitch."

Without saying a word, David hung up and said, "Excuse me for a moment," to Leann, who looked over and smiled.

David got up and turned into the kitchen and closed the door behind him. Chris almost pissed his jeans in anticipation. "It's her, I'm telling you."

"Just keep your voice down," David said, pushing Chris away from the eyehole. "We have got to keep her here as long as possible till I figure out what to do."

"What we do is tie her up in the basement and have some fun," Chris said.

David had to admit it would be nice to take her.

"Don't let your baser instincts get the better of you, fool. She's in our web. The trick is how to attack," David said, wanting to play this move like a chess grand master.

He watched as Leann picked up a four foot by four foot rosewood picture frame and examined it. David's mind could only think, *Here's the bitch who helped take Tracy away from me.*

At that moment Leann walked to the counter with the frame. "Stay here," David said, pushing Chris out of the way.

Opening the door, he said, "May I help you?" gritting his teeth.

"Yes, I would like to purchase this, but I don't see a price."

"For you, pretty lady, forty dollars," he said with death on his lips.

"That's fine. Could you please have it delivered to my address? I don't believe it will fit in my rental car."

"Certainly, but the price goes up ten dollars." David said, reaching for a bill-of-sale slip.

"3218 View Road in Black Eagle," Leann said, still feeling someone was watching her.

"Should arrive within two days," he said.

She handed him the money and said, "Thank you," as he crushed the bills in his hand.

Once she walked out the door, he said, "Checkmate, bitch." He hurried to the front window and pulled the curtain aside. He said, "You can come out now," as he watched her pull into traffic. David had checked the phone book after the ambush and found she was unlisted.

"Why didn't we just grab her?" Chris said, scratching his head.

"You idiot, with her car right outside? No, my friend, we are going to plan this out carefully. I want her to suffer on her way to death," he said, grinning. "We have her address," David said, working his criminal mind to hatch a plan.

Taking the *OPEN* sign from the window and turning it to *CLOSED*, he said, "I have to go out. I'll be back in a couple of hours."

He had a plan. It was something Gregory Cameron had said.

18

Leann made herself comfortable in front of her wooden easel. Having converted a spare bedroom into a painting studio, she felt at peace there. Living in the quiet suburb of Black Eagle, near Great Falls, she relished the easygoing atmosphere and friendly people. She smelled the scent of rain closing in from an open window. Looking out onto her backyard, she watched as two huge willow trees swayed in the wind. "A storm's rolling in," she said.

One hobby she enjoyed was watercolor painting, and she was proud of the fact she was good at it. Most of her home was decorated with Georgia O'Keeffe posters and prints.

A slight chill came over her when she remembered how cold Montana was in the fall and winter. It wasn't for her. She opened a dresser drawer and pulled out a savings account passbook. Her rainy-day account had almost $4,000 in it. She enjoyed looking at it from time to time to remind herself to stay strong, with the goal of moving to the city of angels—Santa Fe, New Mexico—when she had saved enough. She sighed at the prospect of having to put another dream on hold for now.

Checking her watch, she saw it was 6:50 P.M. With dinner almost prepared, she had time before the veal cutlets were done. She sat back down at the easel and tried to come up with an idea for a painting for John.

As she picked up the sable brush, there was a knock at her front door. Praying it wasn't Urbain this early, she made her way through the living room. As she took off her smock, she turned on a lamp and looked through the eyehole. There stood a man with a ponytail, holding a package, with his back to the door.

"Who is it?"

He turned and she could see it was the man from the pawnshop. There was something about the man's dark-brown eyes that caused Leann to back away from the door slightly. Making sure the door was still locked, she said, loud enough so he could hear, "I thought you said it would take two days to deliver."

He did not even blink his eyes or change the expression on his face, Leann thought. "I wanted to delivery this personally," he said with a low-key voice as the rain started to fall, and he still did not blink as it hit his face.

"Thank you for coming. You can leave it outside by the door," she said, afraid to open it.

"I'll need a signature," he said.

Reluctantly she unlocked the door, opening it slightly. She could see he was drenched.

He handed her a clipboard and pen. "Sign here," he said.

Leann wanted him gone and fast. She scrawled her name and grabbed the four by four foot picture frame box from him. There was no way she wanted him in her home.

With a dour face he said, "Hope you enjoy what's in the box," still not even wiping the falling rain from his face. She was afraid he would ask to come in from the rain.

"I am sure I will, thank you," she said with a look that said *I am never going to your shop again*.

Closing the door, she pushed aside her curtains a little to watch him. He walked with a slight limp down her driveway and turned into the street, then almost disappeared into the coming night. As a loud clap of thunder roared, she noticed he did not even flinch. She also thought it strange that he appeared to have no transportation. Then a white cargo van pulled to a stop in front of the man. He got in the driver's side and drove off.

She brought the package into her studio and was about to open it when she stopped. There was a low humming sound. "That must be the wind," she said, setting it upright on an end chair.

She ripped open the pull tab in one quick motion, realizing what the humming was too late. A swarm of bees descended on her. "Oh my God, no!" she said, trying to swat them away. Thinking only of the Epi-Pen that could save her in her purse in the living room, she tried to move. Already stung in the arms and back, she ran to try and get her purse. The effects were overwhelming her senses as she fell in the hallway. Nearly passing out, she managed to crawl into the living room. Reaching for her purse, she emptied the contents, frantically looking for the drug. Finding it, she had only seconds before she lost consciousness.

With the injection still in her hand, she passed out in blackness with the bees in every room, looking for a way out.

19

Seeing Chris, David gave the thumbs-up sign. Chris put the white cargo van in gear and pulled out with a smile on his face. As David climbed into the driver's seat, he said, "I'll drive, move over."

"How'd it go? Any problem?" Chris asked.

"None. When she opens that box with those bees, she's done. That fucking Cameron was good for something after all," David said as they both laughed.

"I know a beekeeper in Great Falls who owed me money, so I told him I'd take two dozen bees instead," David said as he made his way down View Road in the rain. "The hard part was getting them in the box."

"This plan of yours was a stroke of genius," Chris said, combing his blond hair. "What's next?"

"Next is we go after the pilot."

"That reminds me," Chris said, reaching up to the visor for a newspaper. "I took this from someone's driveway when the delivery kid came by. It seems that pilot used drugs in the Air Force. There's even a picture of him. That should hurt his family image. It's all in here in the *Great Falls Tribune* front page news." He tried to show David the story.

"Not while I'm driving, you idiot."

"Sorry," Chris said, folding it back up.

"That's a start, but I want more than bad press. I want his ass in a sling. That's the least we can do for Tracy," David said, glancing at Chris.

Chris knew never to mention her name. It had set David in all sorts of crazy moods.

"You in or out?" David said, speeding over the limit.

"You know I'm in, brother." He was lying as he gently patted David's shoulder. When the pilot was taken care of, his thrill ride with David was over. He smiled as he thought of his next adventure: Canada.

"Fuck everyone," David said as he flipped the bird at a passing pick-up truck.

20

John Urbain, as a general rule, hated dating, but this was no ordinary woman. From what he could tell, Leann was his "it" girl. She was smart and attractive and could handle herself with ease around men.

As he turned onto View Road in Black Eagle, the rain was coming down in torrents. Even with the wipers of his Chevy Silverado going at full tilt, he still had to drive slowly to find her address. The low storm clouds were blocking out what sunlight there was left.

He turned on his headlights and looked at his watch. It showed 7:20 P.M. He smiled at the thought of having dinner with the woman who may be his wife one day. Flashes of lightning streaked across the gray sky, adding to the fading light of sunset.

Dressed in a black Skyway Tours t-shirt, blue jeans, and brown cowboy boots, he hoped to convey an everyday guy look. He ran a free hand through his brown hair and looked at the visor mirror, trying not to be nervous. He was torn between living his own life and adding Leann into the mix. Maybe he was making a mistake. *Just live your life being alone*. Then the thought of a woman's soft touch brought him back to a need that he knew he must fulfill. He smiled, thinking of a home-cooked meal and looking into her bluish-green, cat-like eyes.

Two men in a white cargo van drove by doing 40 in a 25, and gave John the finger. He rolled his window down and gave it right back. "Shake it off. Just two jerks on a Friday night heading to some watering hole," he said.

Coming to the end of a cul-de-sac, he found her address on the mailbox. She lived in a brown-and-white ranch style, 100 feet from the edge of the road. Slipping in behind her Honda Accord, he could see something wasn't right.

"Oh, shit," he said as he saw gray-black smoke coming from all the windows in the rain. He jumped out and made the 20 feet to her front door in under three seconds. He pounded on the door and could make out the smell of burning plastic and grease. Plumes of black and gray smoke were coming from all the windows.

"Leann, can you hear me?" he said as he punched in 911 on his cell phone.

He had to get inside. Looking over at the picture window, he noticed a shaft of light through the open curtain. His heart missed a few beats as he searched for her. There, almost in the middle of the living room, lay Leann.

With his mind racing, he tried to kick the door in. Running to his truck he found a crowbar under the back seat. He beat on the doorknob as the rain grew in intensity.

As the knob broke away, he was able to push the knife edge of the crowbar between the frame and door. He put his full weight into it and the door gave way. Pushing the door aside, breaking one of the hinges, he was met with a swarm of escaping bees. "What the hell," he said, rushing to Leann.

Kneeling beside her, he felt her neck for a pulse. She was breathing, but it was weak. He looked at her hands and saw the EpiPen in her right hand. There was no time to think about it. Making sure that the injection needle was still full, he thrust it into her right thigh through her jeans.

Between the bees and the smoke, he knew he had to move her. Cradling her in his arms, he carried her out to the back seat of his Silverado. "Hang in there, Leann, don't die on me," he said as he put a blanket on her. "Please, God, grant me this," he said as he tried to make her comfortable, praying she would not die.

John ran back in her home hoping to find the source of the smoke. He could only make it to her living room before the thick black fumes pushed him back. It appeared to John to be coming from the kitchen. He was choking on the smoke and barely made it out alive. He fell to his knees on Leann's front lawn and was breathing hard. Thinking only of Leann, he staggered back to his pick-up truck to check on her.

His eyes welled up at the thought of losing her. The tears mixed with the falling rain and added to the moisture that soaked him. *How could this have happened? Bees in her living room and a fire*, he thought. She was alive but non-responsive when he gently tried to wake her. John kissed her forehead and stroked her face, staying with her. *Where's that ambulance?*

Running the questions through his mind, he searched for answers. What would he do if she died? What could he do?

In the distance he could now hear the sirens coming. The thunder clapped once more, sending shock waves that echoed throughout the dark sky.

21

John Urbain awoke on the third floor of the Great Falls Memorial Hospital to a gray, dull sky. Yawning as he stretched in his chair, he looked out of the window that was across from him. The storm had passed and was down to a light drizzle, with heavy, dark-blue clouds rolling east. He looked around and saw that he was the only one in the waiting area.

His mind instantly thought of Leann and how she was doing. Jumping out of the chair, he made his way to the nurses' station and asked about her condition. Told that she was still asleep and he could not see her till after 8 A.M., he walked down to the in-hospital coffee shop.

He was about to enter when a passing nurse who was leaving told her two friends, "There he is, the man who saved her life twice in one week." All eyes turned to John from the dozen or so people who were in the open coffee shop. Some applauded, some booed at John.

"What the hell now?" John asked, turning towards the group.

An elderly man held up a newspaper and said, "Read the first page. There's a nice story of you with a picture."

John could see most of the people were staring at him and wondered why. As the elderly man passed John, he put the newspaper in John's chest and said, "Not such a hotshot now, are you?"

"Leave me alone and go about your business," John said, not in the mood for games this Saturday morning.

Ordering a large black coffee with sugar, he made his way to a booth in the corner. On the front page, he found himself staring at his own picture. There in black and white was the full story of his drug use at Malmstrom AFB years ago with Todd Rudd.

"That little bastard," John said out loud as heads again turned his way.

The story told how he saved a woman's life on Monday and that Mr. Rudd wanted people to know the facts about their "hero." He put both hands to his face and shook his head in disbelief. *The nerve of that little prick*. Not that he thought of himself as a hero; he just would have preferred that part of his past remain hidden to Annie Webster and Leann Blake.

He crumbled up the newspaper and walked over to a trash container, throwing it in with force.

He sipped his coffee and decided to call Ryan Porter. He needed a friend to talk to. Checking the time to see if he would be up, it read 7:35 by his watch. Using his cell, he walked out into the hallway and called Ryan.

"How's tricks?" he asked.

"Hey, what's up?"

After John told him everything that had happened in the last 24 hours, he felt better.

"Man, you sure have a habit of being there when there's trouble with this woman," Ryan said, half asleep.

"What can I say? Have you had a chance to read the newspaper yet?"

"I was wondering when you would get to that. Yeah, I read it. Who the hell is Todd Rudd?"

"It doesn't matter, just a creep I knew in the Air Force. How do you think Annie will react?"

"Hard to say, but it can't be good, in light of the shot-up bird she has to contend with. That plus the fact you once used weed in the Air Force. She hates drugs."

"I know," was all John could say. He hung his head, wishing his drug days hadn't happened. *I guess what goes around, comes around in the end.*

As Ryan asked about Blake, John noticed two nurses were looking his way and whispering to each other. Spotting the newspaper on the desk, he knew why. “So this is how it starts,” he said to them as they turned away.

Ryan asked, “How what starts?”

“I’ll tell you later. Thanks for listening. I’ve got to get going.”

“Hey, man, you okay?” Ryan asked.

“I’m okay.” After saying good-bye, he hung up. He thought about calling Annie but the damage was already done.

The sudden urge for a smoke came over him. Remembering where he was, he knew there wasn’t a cigarette within a mile of the hospital. He wiped his hands over his face and made his way towards the restroom. He needed to splash some cold water on his face before he saw Leann.

Being the only one in there, he took it upon himself for some personal reflection time in the mirror. *What kind of man have I become?* he wondered. Less than a week ago he was happy-go-lucky. Monday changed all that. He thought of Leann. Yes, he’d found a good woman, but at what cost? His job and career were on the line. He looked into the mirror again after rinsing his face a second time. He was beat from having been up all night worried about her. The little sleep he did manage wasn’t enough. And then that bastard Rudd let the cat out of the bag with his exposé. “If I ever see that punk again, I am going to break every bone in his ugly face,” he told himself. Their paths had to cross again. He was sure of it.

He checked his watch. It was 8:03 as he wiped his face with paper towels. If only she could pull through this, he prayed.

Leaving the restroom, he turned towards the elevator as a young couple was passing by. The man asked John if he had smoked any good weed lately. “I don’t do that anymore,” John said, ready to throttle him. The couple laughed at him, then turned and walked away.

After taking the elevator to Leann’s floor, he noticed Detective Dana Lewis outside of her door. “Damn,” he said. He wanted some alone time with her before she read or was told about his drug use. Frowning, he realized a nurse had probably already told her. It sure as hell seemed everyone else knew his past. He made up his mind to come clean with her about everything when they could be alone.

22

Determined to make the best of the situation, John knocked on Leann's door and walked in.

"There's my man," Leann said, surprised he was there this early. John said hello and went to her, kissing her on the cheek. As he pulled away, she grabbed him closer, kissing him on the lips.

"Maybe I should leave you two alone," Detective Lewis said, joking. Sitting in a chair by the window, he smiled at them. "Good to see you both again, under the circumstances," he went on.

John squeezed Leann's hand tenderly and took the chair next to Det. Lewis. John did not even dignify him with a hello. "How are you?" he asked Leann.

"I feel as safe as I can be, with a strong detective and the man who saved my life twice in one week at my side. They're going to run some more tests this afternoon. Bee stings do a huge number on me."

Wanting to explain his visit, Det. Lewis started in. "I was here on another case and I saw your name on the inpatient list. I heard that you were stung by bees and there was a fire. I made some calls to the fire department, and according to them, it was a grease fire that got out of control. The fire was fairly extensive with the smoke and all. Do you have another place you can stay?"

John cleared his throat and said, "She'll be staying with me," as he looked to her for approval.

With a smile that could melt John's heart, she said, "Thank you. I'd feel better having a man around. To think I almost died because of some damn bees."

"What were they doing in your home?" John asked with a suspicious look on his face. "I got stung as I entered," he continued, rolling up his shirtsleeve to show both of them.

Leann ran her hand through her dark hair, collecting her thoughts. "It was that man, the owner of the pawnshop. He delivered a box and when I went to open it, all those bees came at me. He was a very strange man. He must've known I'm allergic to bee stings."

At the mention of a pawnshop, Det. Lewis's ears perked up. "What pawnshop?" he asked as he flipped through his small notebook. Finding the page he wanted, he asked, "Would it be the Longtree Shop in Ulm?" hoping it was another shop entirely.

"How did you know that? Yes, it was," Leann said as she sat up in her bed.

Det. Lewis closed his eyes and shook his head for a moment as he said, "It all comes back to that pawnshop," under his breath.

Reaching into his blue sports jacket, he pulled out a small airline bottle of whiskey. Without looking at either John or Leann, he unscrewed the cap and drank it down in two gulps. "I am off duty." He felt he had to say it to put them both at ease.

Unsure of what to say, John thought it best to get back to the conversation. "What does the pawnshop have to do with Leann?" he asked.

"Did you tell Gregory Cameron you were allergic to bees?" Det. Lewis asked Leann.

"Yeah. You know, he used to make jokes about it."

"Considering you almost died, I fail to see the humor," Det. Lewis said with a stony face.

"I still don't see the connection between Leann and the pawnshop. Could you enlighten both of us?" John said, growing impatient.

After tossing the empty bottle into the wastebasket from across the room, Det. Lewis drew a deep breath. "Here's what we know so far," he said, flipping through his notebook. "Leann, you were on your way to Bozeman to turn in some SARs and CTRs, right?"

"That's right. I've made that trip a dozen times. What are you driving at?" she answered.

"She's the assistant bank manager. It's part of her job," John said, feeling the need to defend her.

"Please, let me explain," Det. Lewis said, trying to tie up some loose ends of the investigation in his mind. "The last phone call the late Miss Tracy Burke made was to that pawnshop. I found Mr. Gregory Cameron's number in her private phone book. I believe she was a prostitute he was using on the sly. The owner of the pawnshop, Mr. David Longtree, called in a stolen vehicle that was used in the ambush. The dead man, Lamar Singleton, was employed there."

"What does—" John asked, but Det. Lewis waved him off, continuing.

"Your boss, Cameron, has turned up missing according to his wife, who filed a report yesterday."

"Oh my God, do you think he was involved with all of this?" Leann asked in a loud voice.

"Yes, I do but I can't prove it…yet," Det. Lewis said. "Have you been to that pawnshop before, Miss Blake?" he asked her.

"No, yesterday was the first time, I swear."

"I believe you. But of all the places to go, you unwittingly went to the shop that is involved with the accident you had."

"What are you getting at? You saying Leann had something to do with this—the accident, the bees?" John asked, growing more angry by the minute.

"She *is* involved. I think she plays a part in it by her job. Cameron knew you would be driving to Bozeman, correct?"

"Yes," Leann said, afraid of where this was heading.

Det. Lewis was writing notes down faster than he could think. "Something stinks at that pawnshop, and I think it's the owner,

Longtree," he said. "There's too many questions. And you say he was the one to make the delivery to your home?" he asked Leann, already knowing the answer.

"Yes, it was the owner."

John, now standing, asked, "You think Cameron and Longtree were in on the bees? But why?"

"I believe Longtree was laundering money from Tracy's affairs in your bank, Leann. Cameron was in on it. That's why there are no copies of those reports at Northwest State Bank on Riverside Drive."

"He's a weird sort of guy, but I never imagined he was capable of that," she said, looking at Det. Lewis with a surprised face.

"Desperate men do desperate things, I'm afraid."

"Do you think he was receiving kickbacks from Longtree?" John asked.

"I'm sure he was but I doubt I'll ever be able to prove it," Det. Lewis said.

"So why the bees?" John asked.

"Plain and simple, the hard truth is it's revenge for Burke and Singleton's deaths. Mr. Longtree has a long list of criminal activity in his family history. I checked. But he's never been implicated."

"Till now," John said, hoping there was something they could nail him on.

"All I have is circumstantial evidence so far. I'll keep looking," Det. Lewis said, smiling, sure he would be able to arrest Longtree at some point.

Raising his voice, John said, "I'll get to the bottom of this mess. Give me time alone with this Longtree dude. I'll get the answers you need."

"You don't want to do that," Det. Lewis said, feeling anger coming on. He didn't care for people implying he couldn't do his job.

"I'll do whatever it takes to protect her, and it appears you've done nothing but take notes," John said, moving closer to him.

Pointing a finger at John, he said, "If you interfere with this case,

I'll have you arrested." John broke out in a smile and said nothing. "Don't think I won't," Det. Lewis added for good measure.

Turning to Leann, he said, "Miss Blake, I'll keep in touch. And Mr. Urbain, you heard what I said. Stay out of it and let the police do their job."

"The way I look at it, Longtree tried twice to kill Leann. There will be a third attempt. You think about that, Detective," John said as he moved to Leann's side.

"Let us do our job. Good day," Det. Lewis said as he left the room.

"I don't like it. They hurt you and very well may have lost me my job." He fell silent, remembering that Leann didn't know. Before she could say anything, he sat back down and told her about Todd Rudd, the drugs, and the newspaper article. After he was done, he felt like he was on trial, awaiting a verdict.

She smiled and said, "It doesn't change anything." She patted her bed for him to sit next to her. "Fate brought us together, and love will keep us together."

John smiled and leaned in to kiss her, now sure she was the woman he was looking for. "Hold that thought, babe. I need to apologize to Det. Lewis. I'll be right back."

"I'll be here."

Making his way down the crowded hallway towards the elevator, John could see Det. Lewis waiting. "I'm glad I was able to catch up with you. I would like to apologize for the way I acted back there."

Det. Lewis smiled and said, "I know you're both frustrated. I'll tell you what," he said, rubbing his chin, "I'm going out to the pawnshop tomorrow morning. How about coming along? I'll square it with my boss. I'll even pick you up at your place."

"That would be great. I'll look forward to it," John said, extending his hand.

Det. Lewis clasped John's hand in a firm handshake. "See you tomorrow then," he said as the elevator doors swung open.

23

David was dreaming of Tracy. He could see her bloodied face. She was trying to say something, but he could not make out what. The image grew smaller. She was fading away from him, all the time shaking her head back and forth. He tried to reach out to hold her but could not reach her. She faded to darkness. He thought he heard the words, "Don't do it, sweetie. Don't do it."

As it went from a dream to a nightmare, he could hear another voice urging him to wake up. "Wake up, dude, wake up." He slowly lost the image of Tracy to blackness, but could still hear "wake up." It seemed he was being shaken. Then, with a start, he opened his eyes, drenched in sweat, to see Chris Fields over him holding a newspaper.

"What the hell do you want?" David said, pissed off but glad he was awake. There were too many nights of imagining Tracy being thrown through the windshield in his nightmares.

"We got a problem. She's alive," Chris said, still standing above him.

As David rubbed his eyes and sat up in his bed, he asked, "Who? Who's alive?"

"That bitch, the one who was here, Leann Blake," Chris said, louder than David would have liked to hear. "Read this," Chris said, shoving the newspaper article in David's face.

David grabbed the newspaper, still trying to shake the cobwebs from his troubled mind. In bold, huge, black letters he saw the words **PILOT SAVED WOMAN TWICE,** and underneath the headline **LEANN BLAKE RESCUED FROM BEE STINGS AND**

HOUSE FIRE. Those words brought David awake like a splash of cold water.

As David read the article as fast as he could, he said, "I don't believe it. Where did that bastard come from? She was alone when we left." Then the picture of them giving the finger to a man in a pick-up truck sprang into his head.

"There was nobody around. She lives on an empty cul-de-sac. It must have been that prick in the Silverado we passed," David said as he threw the paper across the bedroom.

"What do we do now?" Chris said as he took a chair next to David's bed.

David knew at that moment it was over. The police would be sniffing around asking all sorts of questions, this time about the damn bees. *Yes*, he thought, *it is truly over*. All his hopes and dreams flew away, like Tracy through the windshield.

Self-preservation kicked in, David thought like a tidal wave. "What we do is get the hell out of here, and fast," David said, throwing the covers aside and hopping out of bed. "I'm going to the cabin," he said, already thinking what he needed to pack. He would not be coming back.

"So we run away with our tails between our legs?" Chris said, now standing. "I'm not running. I'm sick of all of this shit. Fucking let them come. I'll pick them off one by one," Chris said, pointing a finger like a gun at imaginary police figures. "We should never have done it, the ambush and all," he said.

"But we did do it and now we pay the price. Well, I'll tell you, I am not sticking around to have a firefight with law enforcement like the OK Corral, that's for sure," David said, already throwing clothes from his dresser onto his bed to be packed. Heading over to his closet, he continued, "If you want to stay, that's up to you, but color me gone."

"No, I'm going to stay. I have no place else to go with Lamar and Tracy gone…" Chris said as he sat back down again on the chair, resigning himself to life's end.

David was not even listening. He was thinking of how much money he had around the shop and what firearms he could take with him. If the end was coming, he wanted it to be at his cabin near Holter Lake, Montana. A tear came to his eyes as he thought of all the times he spent there with Tracy. *What do I care about Chris? If he hadn't involved Tracy she would still be alive.*

As he opened a suitcase to throw his clothes in he thought of dying. No, he wasn't going to go yet, not without taking Leann and that pilot along for death's ride.

The image of his father and grandfather running from the police popped into his head. Then there was Carl, his older brother, who had also fled when police closed in. "No way I am going to prison," David said to himself, as Chris had already left the room.

After emptying his safe of cash, two Smith & Wesson .45s with ammo, and other valuables, David Longtree was almost ready to leave. Making his way back to his bedroom, he closed the door behind him and locked it. Reaching with one hand under his bed, he pulled out a prized possession that even Fields did not know he had: a black, metal gun case with an AK-47 inside with four clips, 30 rounds in each. He had bought it off a sergeant at Malmstrom AFB who was looking for some quick cash.

David picked up the case and unlocked the door. Opening it slowly, he looked to see if Chris was around. Figuring he was still downstairs cleaning his .45s and sharpening his Bowie knife, David moved quickly to get to the trunk of his Ford Explorer. *Maybe make my way south towards Texas*, he thought as he slammed the trunk down, *after spending some time at the cabin*. He desperately needed some alone time to collect his thoughts and come up with a plan. No way he was going to leave Blake and Urbain alive to spend their days growing old together. "Retribution is its own reward," he said under his breath as he stepped back into the pawnshop.

"Chris, I'm ready to go," he yelled downstairs.

Chris hurried up the stairs and said, "So this is it," with a look of disdain.

"What else can I do? I can't take you with me in case someone recognizes you," David said, lying. He just felt it was time to cut ties with Chris. The hell with him.

"Whatever happens, don't tell anyone where I am at. You owe me that much," he continued, knowing full well if law enforcement did come, Chris would end up in a body bag on his way to the city morgue.

David did not want to, but he stuck out his hand. Chris slapped his hand away and pulled him close for a back-slapping bear hug. "Stay cool, dude, and don't let that bastard win," Chris said as he turned away from David.

"Oh, by the way, dude, thanks for taking me in," Chris said, not looking at David. With his back to him, he said, heading back downstairs, "If I can, I am going to make my way to Canada. I've got some money saved."

"Stay cool," was all David could say, after three years together with him, Lamar, and Tracy living the dream. *What a difference a week makes*, David thought as he turned to leave the pawnshop.

The cabin at Holter Dam was less than an hour away. *I've got to go underground for a while, but I'll be back*, he vowed to himself. He did not worry about Chris Fields. The police would see to that. One thing he could say about Chris was he would go down fighting. More important, he'd keep his trap shut.

24

John Urbain could not sleep, so he sat on the front steps of his home in Sun Prairie, a light blue with white trim, two-bedroom ranch style, with his black Labrador, Prowler, at his side. He sat, shirtless, in only a faded pair of blue jeans, with a hot cup of black coffee. He watched the sky come to life with the morning sunrise. Prowler rested his head on John's knee and tried to fall asleep. John looked towards the eastern sky as the reddish-orange sun peeked above the suburban rooftops.

"What a difference a week makes," he said to the dog, who opened his eyes and yawned.

Urbain loved flying, especially this time of the morning, with the mist in low-lying areas burning away with each passing hour. The Montana summer colors were in full bloom, and he missed the view from above.

The sweet face of Leann Blake came into his mind. He had to remember to pick up some flowers, like daisies, bluebells, and golden asters, to give his home a female touch. She would like that. He smiled as he thought of her. One week ago he was alone with no one, and later this afternoon he was taking her home from the hospital to live with him. He'd have plenty of time to settle in with her as he more than likely was unemployed.

He thought of calling Annie Webster and checked his watch. The time was 7:15 and, being a Sunday, he thought the better of it. It would have to wait till Monday. Either way, he would need to update his resume and check the Internet for job openings.

He stretched his arms out and felt a twinge of pain in his left shoulder.

✣ ✣ ✣

As John looked at his wound in the bathroom mirror, he wondered if he should take another 10 mg of OxyContin to ease the pain. He also wanted to take the edge off. He decided against it.

There was one thing he could do as he waited for Detective Lewis to show up. Going to his bedroom closet, underneath some folded dress shirts he found what he was searching for. He pulled down an aluminum gun case, which had a stainless steel .357 Ruger revolver with a four-inch barrel. He opened the case to check and see if it was loaded; it was, with six shots. He took out the conceal-and-carry permit and tucked it in his wallet. Whoever this owner Longtree was, he didn't care. He was determined to protect himself and Leann Blake.

Adjusting the shoulder holster, he felt the pain return. He did a succession of quick draws to gauge his response time. Wincing, he drew and pointed with both hands on the grip. He was slower than he would have liked but faster than he thought he would be. He tried three more times with the same result.

With pain, he removed the shoulder holster and put on a dark-blue t-shirt. The shoulder harness strapped back on, it felt nice and snug but hurt like hell. He chose a black tweed jacket to hide the gun. He had to admit he looked good, dressed up with his hair combed back. "Just in case," he said to himself as he made his way to the kitchen for another cup of coffee.

The sight of an unmarked detective's car pulling into his driveway caught his attention. He could hear Prowler barking from his cage out back. After quieting the dog, he reached his front door as Detective Lewis was about to knock. John said hello and noticed the detective's .45-caliber Glock pistol in his belt holster. With his brown Stetson hat, brown sports jacket, and dark tanned cowboy boots, he looked like the quintessential Western detective.

"And where do you think you're going with that?" he said to John.

"I've got a permit," John shot back, feeling defensive.

"I want to see it," Det. Lewis said with a dry smirk.

After looking it over, he handed it back to John and said, "Fine, but you stay in the car, understand? I'll fill you in after I've talked to Longtree."

"You're the boss," John said, feeling a sense of admiration towards the 48-year-old detective.

✤ ✤ ✤

As they took the on-ramp to Interstate 15 heading west into Ulm, John asked about the blond-haired man. Det. Lewis shook his head. "He seems to have disappeared into thin air. No tracks or fingerprints, only the reporter's pictures, which are grainy at best. I asked the FBI to take a look at them. We'll find him. He's bound to show up or make a mistake.

"You and Miss Blake seem to be hitting it off," he continued.

"Yeah, she's a good woman," John said, staring straight ahead, wanting him to change the subject.

As he watched the rolling landscape and billboards zip by, his thoughts came back to Leann. *Why do I feel this way? I should be glad about finding her. Maybe I blame her for possibly losing my job.* He guessed it came down to which he wanted more—Leann or flying. He knew only time would tell. Anyway, it sure as hell was not her fault. Both the detective and John were silent till they pulled into the lot.

Det. Lewis said, "Here it is. Now stay in the car. Let me handle it. Got it?"

John nodded his consent. "What a shabby-looking establishment." The parking lot was in need of a new repaving from the potholes. The white paint had faded to yellow on the building. It was also chipped and worn. There were bald tires stacked in two rolls next to the front door. A rusted-out air conditioner was mounted on top of the tires. *The city of Ulm should condemn this hole*, John thought.

Det. Lewis said, "I've seen worse, but not by much." He opened his door and said to John, "Smile and wave," as he pointed to the camera that was aimed at them from the roof.

John watched as Det. Lewis adjusted his Stetson, walked to the front door and knocked. He saw the *CLOSED* sign in the window. John rolled down his window and said, "Looks like nobody's home."

"I'll check around back," Det. Lewis said, making his way to the south side of the building. He walked along a chipped and uneven sidewalk that led to the back of the building. It passed beneath a three-car overhead canopy. The cement trail was strewn with weeds and dandelions. The canopy housed one old white cargo van, like the one used in the ambush. He looked in the dirty windows but saw nothing of interest.

Continuing up the sidewalk, he noticed an open window to his right. As he got closer he could smell coffee brewing. Cupping his hands to block out the glare, he looked inside the window. Making out what appeared to be a small kitchen, one object caught his attention: a Smith & Wesson .45 caliber lying on a table in the center of the room. Instinct took over as he reached to his side and undid the strap to his gun.

He moved against the side of the building so as to not be seen by someone if they came into the kitchen. With coffee brewing on the stove and a .45 in the open, someone had to be home.

He inched closer to the edge to look around to the other side. Who was home? The owner or even the tall, blond-haired man was a definite possibility.

Before he turned the corner, he drew his Glock, holding it up with both hands on the grip.

As he turned the corner, he was met with a Bowie knife to his upper left chest from a tall, blond-haired man. Det. Lewis stumbled backward as the man tried to grab his gun from him. With all of his strength, he squeezed off one round that nicked the man in his right shoulder. The man wrestled the gun away as Det. Lewis fell to his knees. The man smiled and leveled the gun at Det. Lewis. "Time to blow your head off, you old fool. Say your prayers, pig, then you die."

Det. Lewis put his hands up in a defensive position as a shot rang out from behind the man. The man looked at his chest as a pool of blood was forming on his white t-shirt. He looked at the detective with surprise, was about to say something, then rolled his eyes and fell face first onto the sidewalk.

Standing in a crouched position at the other end of the building was John Urbain. His hands were shaking as he slowly put his Ruger .357 to his side. He ran up to kick the gun away from the man and felt his neck for a pulse. There was none.

He pulled out his cell phone and dialed 911. The detective winked at him as he told the dispatcher, "Officer down, the Longtree pawnshop in Ulm, send back-up and an ambulance."

"You decided not to listen to me after all. Good thing too, otherwise I'd be dead," the detective said, trying to laugh with blood coming from his mouth.

John rolled the blond-haired man over. "That's the man I saw from the helicopter."

"Watch that door until help arrives. If anybody else is inside, they know we're here," the detective said, trying to point to the back door.

John nodded and drew his weapon as he opened the screen door and darted to the kitchen door. He listened for any movement, keeping the .357 in front of him and walking slowly through the kitchen out into the display area. *If anyone was in here they would have high-tailed it out the front door by now.* he assured himself. Taking small steps, he was scared as he pressed onward. All of his senses were acutely aware that someone, anyone could appear out of nowhere and take a shot.

Checking both bedrooms and the downstairs, he found he was alone. Putting his gun away, he went to the front counter and scanned the assortment of snapshots pinned to a bulletin board. He focused on trying to find one that looked like he might be the owner. A four by six inch color picture that read *David Longtree* caught his eye. A man with a ponytail stood outside of a hunting cabin in a Montana winter holding a rifle in one hand. The other was giving the finger. The picture was dated a few years ago. The cabin looked like it was near Holter Lake. John knew the area well, having gone fishing there.

He took the picture down, removed the frame, and stuffed the picture under his shirt. He knew he should give it to the police for evidence of where Longtree might be. He couldn't do it. If Longtree would try to hurt Leann again, John was going to find him himself.

In the distance he could hear sirens coming. He walked through the kitchen to the back door. "All clear; there's no sign of Longtree," he told the detective.

"Maybe we can find you a job on the force after this is over. I wish you hadn't gone in, though, good job. And thank you."

John looked over at the pool of blood under the man he had killed. He got sick to his stomach. Dropping to his knees, he vomited twice and turned away.

"Naw, once is enough for me," he said with his hands still shaking.

Where is Longtree?

25

John Urbain had never seen so many police, state patrol, and unmarked squads in his life. It seemed the whole of the police force had shown up from Great Falls and beyond. When one of their own went down, everyone showed up to help. They were sad that Detective Lewis was knifed, but you could see the smiles on their face that the perpetrator was dead. Almost every officer and detective was patting John on the back. He just felt like throwing up again.

Before Det. Lewis was taken to Great Falls Hospital, he gave a statement clearing John of any wrongdoing. They kept his gun for evidence till the district attorney had a chance to review the case.

With the mystery of the blond-haired man out of the way, John felt better, but not by much, with the owner still on the loose. There was no warrant out on David Longtree, but the police would still like to talk to him.

Remembering he still had to pick up Leann, John checked his watch. There was time if he hurried. After giving his statement to law enforcement, he was free to go. An officer offered him a ride home as a white station wagon from the morgue pulled into the lot.

✤ ✤ ✤

David Longtree was just pulling into the long cul-de-sac driveway of his cabin when the first reports came over his police scanner. "I hope at least the cop dies," he said to himself as he unloaded his Ford Explorer. The thought of Tracy came to his mind as he opened the cabin door and the smell of sandalwood incense filled his nose. The memory of the last time he was there caused him to throw the suitcase across the kitchen.

"Fucking bastard pilot!" he yelled and it echoed throughout. He made his way towards the bedroom and could see the flowers he had picked for her, dead and wilted on the nightstand.

He slumped in an old rocking chair and stared out the window at the tall pine trees that were swaying back and forth. Faces of the dead filled his mind. He closed his eyes.

Tracy Burke

Lamar Singleton

Gregory Cameron

Chris Fields

He rocked back and forth to his heartbeat. Beads of sweat formed on his brow.

"You were right," he said to himself as the image of his father, who always said he would amount to nothing, burned into his mind.

He opened his eyes and saw the gun case on his bed. The thought of resting the rifle under his chin and squeezing the trigger crossed his mind. He couldn't go back to the pawnshop with the whole police force looking for him. He was trapped and alone. *Maybe I could run to Canada*, he thought.

No. He was tired of running away. *I've still got work to do in killing that pilot and Blake.*

He grasped the armrests tightly as he speculated about Leann Blake and the pilot. If only he hadn't shown up at the ambush. Longtree clenched his teeth at the thought of the pilot being a local hero.

David was already the murderer of Gregory Cameron. What would one or two more matter?

As it started to rain, he took a deep breath and smiled. He closed his eyes and rocked himself to sleep.

He had a plan.

26

The scent of rain filled the warm summer air as the police officer pulled into John Urbain's lot in Sun Prairie. As he walked up his driveway, he looked towards the west and could see flashes of lightning among the approaching dark clouds. Seven seconds later he heard the rumble.

In all the excitement, he had developed a massive headache. All he wanted to do was let Prowler out to do his business, take some aspirin, and lie on his bed with a cool washcloth draped across his forehead.

He opened the back door. Prowler was waiting to be let out. John stepped aside and let the dog slide by, wagging his tail. He made his way to the bathroom for a couple of aspirin when he remembered he had to pick up Leann soon. He frowned at the thought of having to entertain anyone just now. *Of all the days for me to take another man's life, it had to be today*, he thought. *The man deserved it, but still, killing a human being wasn't an easy thing to do. Or to live with.*

As he strolled to his bedroom, he took out the picture of Longtree from underneath his t-shirt. He sat on the edge of his bed and stared at the man with the ponytail. The cold, dead-set eyes and a smile that said *come and get me if you can* while flipping him the finger caused all of John's muscles to tighten.

John thought better of crushing the picture in his hands. He reached over, tossed it in his bedside table drawer, and slammed it shut with a thud. *If the police don't find you, I will,* he said to himself as he stretched out on his bed, closed his eyes, and listened to the rain.

He dozed off for five minutes before his cell phone vibrated with an incoming call. It was Leann. "Hello, John. If you're okay with me staying with you, I'll be discharged in about an hour. You still up for this?" she asked. Her voice was happy, upbeat, and was a tonic to John's ears. He thought her voice had a soothing effect on him.

"Sure, I'll be there in an hour," he said, even as his head was only slightly pounding now. He wondered, *How am I going to tell her that I had to kill a man today?*

Pushing the thought from his mind, he spent the next 20 minutes making sure his home was neat and orderly for her. He'd stop and buy some nice flowers on his way to the hospital. But no blood-red roses. He had seen enough red for one day.

Satisfied that all was well for Leann, he rounded up Prowler and corralled him into his cage in the backyard as the rain subsided for the moment.

The instant he jumped into his Silverado, his phone went off. He looked at the number and said, "And here it comes." It was Annie Webster.

John debated if he should answer it or not. He took a deep breath and said, "Hello, Annie, what can I do for you this Sunday afternoon?" He closed his eyes as she said the words that he dreaded to hear.

"I am sorry, John, but after reading the article in the newspaper and doing a lot of soul-searching, I've decided to terminate your employment with Skyway Tours and Transport. It was a hard decision to make, but I have to do it." His headache returned and he developed a twist in his stomach as she went on and on. "I mean, how can I ever trust you again? Are you using drugs now?"

"No, it was a long time ago, I was…"

"Spare me the reasons why or how long ago. The bottom line is you've flown your last flight with this company. I'll have Ryan clean out your locker and send you the stuff. Please don't come to the shop anymore."

"So that's it? You're firing me by phone on a Sunday? Give me a break," John said, unable to control his frustration.

"I'll send a bill for the damage to the Bell, and your..."

"The hell with the damage," he interrupted, "I own almost a fourth of that company."

"John, I think you need help."

"Don't play psychiatrist with me, okay? It was my flying that put Skyway on the map," John said, trying to win a losing argument.

"It's still my company and I'll hire and fire whom I like. I'll give you a good recommendation if you choose to continue flying. You better hope your shares pay for my chopper. Good-bye, John." She hung up.

If I choose to? What choice do I have? he thought.

John looked at the phone in disbelief and tossed it over to the passenger seat. He gripped the steering wheel with all the force he could muster. "Son of a bitch, that bastard Rudd," he said as he started the engine and backed out of the driveway. As he peeled out, he left a haze of blue smoke behind him.

Suddenly the image of Walter Clark and Todd Rudd, smiling and giving each other high fives, filled his mind. He had to apply his brakes when he looked at his speedometer. He was 20 miles over the speed limit in a residential neighborhood.

John's mind was as reckless as his driving. *That nutcase Longtree is still out there. I had to kill a man to save a man. I owe a wheelbarrow of money to Annie for damages. And thanks to that creep Todd Rudd, I am out of a job.* He wondered if it could get any worse.

He smiled as a clap of thunder startled him and the rain came down in waves once again. "Easy, John," he said to himself as he tried to gain his composure. He took slow, deep breaths as he made the on-ramp to the interstate, heading into Great Falls.

27

John Urbain took the off-ramp at Central Avenue, crossing the Missouri River into downtown Great Falls. He did not have time to pick up flowers for Leann, thanks to Annie's call. Turning off 13th Avenue and into Great Falls Memorial Hospital, he saw Leann waiting under the emergency entrance canopy. She was wearing the same black halter top and jeans. John smiled. She looked great, even in the rain.

He honked his horn to get her attention, pulling alongside her. She waved and climbed in. "Well, hello there. I was beginning to think you changed your mind," she said, brushing the hair from her eyes.

John leaned into her and kissed her. Leann's bluish-green eyes opened wide as she moved closer to him. "What's that for?"

John put the truck into drive and said, "You're the best part of an otherwise bad day."

"Why? What happened?"

"I'll tell you later. How are you doing?"

"The doctor says I'll be fine and to avoid bees."

"Are you up for something to eat?"

"I'm starved. That would be great," she said, putting her arm around him.

John didn't know where he was going to go; he just wanted to be far away from the hospital. The thought of Detective Lewis being rushed into surgery was too much for him. John's face turned flush as he pulled out of the lot, heading anywhere but here.

"Something's wrong. Your face is turning red," she said with a dour grin.

"Hold that thought," he said as he spotted a Denny's restaurant up ahead on his left. He punched the gas pedal, just beating a red light, and said, "Sometimes, Leann, you have to take a chance, and by the way, you look great."

"Easy, babe. We've both seen enough of the hospital for a while, and thank you."

"You're right, I am sorry," he said as he pulled into Denny's and found a space in front by the door.

John bolted out and ran around to her side to open the door for her. "My hero," she said as she stepped out. They held hands and sprinted to the door to escape the rain.

Walking in, John saw the place was nearly empty. He wanted a booth away from people. John took Leann's hand and made his way past the *Please Wait To Be Seated* sign as a waitress followed them. He pointed to a secluded booth across from the kitchen and they slid in facing each other.

The waitress stood at the center of the table and asked, "What can I get you?"

John looked at her name tag that read *Jennie* and said, "Two coffees to start."

"Make mine a decaf tea," Leann said, looking at John with a straight face.

John looked up at the 30-something waitress with blond hair pulled back and said, "Make mine strong and black." As she started to write, John reached over to Leann and grabbed her hand, warm and soft, one of those things that make a woman a woman. John smiled.

The waitress handed them each a menu and turned away, saying, "You don't see people holding hands anymore."

Leann turned towards her, saying, "Well, we plan on holding hands a lot," as she winked at John.

John shot back, "You're a strange woman, Leann."

"Not really. I just believe in being up front. Now please tell me about your day."

"Order first," John said, pulling his hand away to scan the menu.

In an instant John could tell Leann was impatient. "Easy, Leann. Let me collect my thoughts," he said, not taking his eyes off the menu.

Jennie the waitress came back and set the beverages down in front of them. Hovering over them both, she asked, "Are you ready to order yet?"

Gesturing towards Leann, he said, "Ladies first." He watched her skim the menu and admired her figure—curves in all the right places.

"I'll have scrambled eggs, ham, toast, milk, and some OJ, please," she said, putting the menu aside. "You deserve a hero sandwich after what you did," Leann said, looking into John's eyes.

Looking up at the waitress, he said, "I'll have the same," handing her the menus and ignoring the comment.

The waitress stood there and asked Leann, "What did he do?"

John shook his head at Leann to say, *Don't go there*.

She shot a perplexed look back at him and said, "Let's just say he was there when I needed him."

The waitress took the menus and said, glancing at him, "Good for you," and turned and walked away. She muttered, "Back in two shakes."

When the waitress was out of earshot, John leaned in close to Leann and whispered, "I went with Detective Lewis to the pawnshop. There was a shot. Detective Lewis was down with a knife in his chest. I shot the blond-haired man from the ambush. He's dead."

"Oh my God! Are you okay? What happened?"

He told her the whole story, with his hands shaking a little. He relived the incident in his mind and started to perspire. When he was done he leaned back with a blank look in his eyes, staring at her.

"I can't believe it, but you had to do it," she said with eyes wide. He could see she was in mild shock mode now. "I remember throwing coffee into his face, then I passed out."

The waitress returned with the food. They both picked at it, unsure on how to proceed. Leann looked up at him and asked, "Maybe I should take a hotel for a couple of days?"

He put down his fork slowly and looked into her moist eyes. “There’s no need fôr that. I’ll work through this in my own way. I would like you to move in with me.”

“I don’t know what’s going to happen between us, but I know you’re a good man, John Urbain.”

“Maybe not as good as you think. There’s something else I’ve got to tell you. My boss called today to say I’m fired because I lied on my application.”

“This has been a bad day for you. What did you lie about?” she said, running her hands through her long dark hair.

He was reluctant to tell her. He turned away from her and watched the raindrops slowly slide down the window next to the booth. “I used pot when I was in the Air Force, right at Malmstrom AFB,” he said, now ashamed. “It was a long time ago.”

He could see a smile form on her face. “Is that all? You already told me this at the hosipital. We all make mistakes, babe. We’ll get by this.” Clearing her throat, she reached over and touched his hands, stroking them gently. “As long as we’re playing confession, I have something I need to tell you.”

John took a forkful of eggs and washed them down with coffee. “It can’t be any worse than what I told you.”

Leann still picked at her food slowly. He could see something was troubling her.

She readied herself and came out with it. “I was married before I met you. He’s a trial lawyer in upstate New York. I was young and foolish and in my twenties. We were married two years in Cody, my hometown.”

John said nothing. He just continued to finish his plate and nod.

Leann continued, “It’s a good thing we didn’t have children. He was never home anyway.”

Folding her hands in front of her, she went on. “I find it hard to trust men. I am not looking for white picket fences and children. In fact, I can’t have any.”

“Leann, I can’t fault you for something that happened a long time ago. It seems our past can come back to haunt us. As far as kids go, I'm not into children or having a family," he said, pushing his plate away. "I thought you were hungry. Eat, Leann."

She wiped her brow and said, "I am glad I got that off my chest."

"And a nice chest it is. You look sexy in that top," John said in a whisper so only Leann could hear.

"Stop it or I'll blush," she said, laughing.

John winked and smiled.

He saw her dig into her ham and eggs and devour her plate with a profound smile. When she shoved her plate away, he asked, "Do you like dogs?"

"Not really. Why?"

"I have a black Labrador called Prowler. I think you two will hit it off," he said as he waved for the waitress.

"We'll see."

Leann looked out the window. "Oh look, the rain has stopped, and the sun is peeking through. Maybe there's a rainbow."

As they got up to leave, John remarked, "In Montana, anything is possible."

Try as he might, he couldn't push the thought of Longtree out of his mind.

28

John Urbain awoke next to Leann, remembering a night of passionate lovemaking. The best he'd had in quite some time. As she slept facing him, he stroked her face. It was soft and warm. He watched her sleep and thought of the countless nights he'd spent alone. So far they got along fine, and he considered Leann his "it" girl. He leaned in close and smelled her hair. It had the faint hint of peach and clover. Her right leg was on top of the blanket, long and shapely, the way he liked it. He grinned at the prospect of sharing life together as one.

The room was filled with the soft glow of early morning. With the windows open, he felt a cool breeze and could hear birds chirping. The smell of pine trees that lined his lot was in the air.

He looked at Prowler, who was staring at him from an easy chair across the room. John could sense he was in a sullen mood with the arrival of Leann to his domain. John slowly shook his head at the dog as if to say, *Get used to it.* Prowler leapt off the chair and left the room. *He'll come around*, John thought.

He gently rolled out of bed to make coffee and let the dog out. He looked again at Leann as he put on a pair of gray sweat pants and socks. She was still sleeping soundly.

He crept out of the room and down the hall to the kitchen. Prowler was waiting at the back door. "You want out, boy?" he asked as the dog wagged his tail even faster in anticipation.

Letting the dog out, John took in the view of the sky. Light, puffy clouds were rolling in after yesterday's rainstorm. He strolled to the front door to get the newspaper. He wanted to read an update on Detective Lewis and the incident that unfolded at the pawnshop.

He found it on the second page as he went back to the kitchen to make coffee. As he filled the coffeemaker, he heard Leann come down the hallway.

He looked up at her as she said, "Good morning. I hope you don't mind."

John could only smile and look at her from her black hair down to her toes. She was wearing one of his long-sleeved white dress shirts and white socks. She looked like a sexy angel.

Without saying a word, he put down the newspaper, walked towards her, putting his arms around her waist, and kissed her. "Good morning, angel. How'd you sleep?" he asked with a sheepish grin.

She smiled back. "I think you already know the answer to that question."

"Yeah, I think I do. Coffee's up in five minutes," he said, handing her a cup, smiling.

"Great. That gives me time to take a shower, if you don't mind."

"Not at all, help yourself."

"You're a sweetheart," she said, turning towards the bathroom.

He waited till she closed the door and turned on the water. He didn't want to say anything about the newspaper article or the thought of Longtree out there somewhere. What were his intentions? Where was he? John looked at the story again and said, "I'd feel better if I knew Leann was safe." He tossed the newspaper on the counter as he waited for the coffee to brew.

He was about to sit on a kitchen chair when his cell phone chirped an incoming call. He picked it up off the counter, not recognizing the area code. "Hello?"

"Is this John Urbain?"

"Yes, who's calling?"

"Hello, this is Robert Tyre of Helio Tours out of Santa Fe, New Mexico, calling to see if you'd be interested in coming down for an interview."

"How did you get my number?" John asked.

"The same way everyone does—we looked in a Great Falls phone book. I'll admit it took a little digging, but our company has extensive resources."

John sat down, interested in what Mr. Tyre had to offer.

"We read about your exploits in the local paper and online. I think we could use you if you'd be willing to relocate to New Mexico."

John wanted to be upfront and honest this time around and said, "My current employer let me go for lying about drug use years ago on my application."

"Really?" Mr. Tyre said and then paused as if writing a note to himself. John could feel his hopes fading away. "You don't use drugs now, do you?"

"No, no, it was a long time ago, and I regret it every day. My FAA physical and pilot's certification are up to date," he added.

"When would you be available to come down for a chat with me and my senior staff?"

Surprised they would still consider him, John said, "I can be there tomorrow if need be."

"Excellent. Take my number and call me personally when you arrive. I'll pick you up at the airport and we'll do lunch."

"Sounds great. I have your number on my cell, and I'll call you when I get there," John said.

"I'll see you then."

"Thank you," John said with a lump in his throat.

After hanging up, John sat back and wondered how this would all play out as Leann was getting dressed in his bedroom. He didn't like the idea of leaving Leann alone. Maybe she could accompany him on the trip. He knew she had always wanted to live there. *Now, that's what I would call a strange twist of fate.*

He heard her coming down the hallway. When she entered the kitchen, she looked great. John caught a whiff of her; she smiled and poured herself a coffee. "You smell fantastic," he said as she pulled out a chair and looked at him.

"Thanks. The shower helped to bring me around," she said as she took a sip.

"I heard you talking. Who was on the phone?" she asked.

"I just got a job interview, but there's a small problem."

"Tell me."

"It's in Santa Fe, New Mexico, and they want me there tomorrow."

Her cat-like eyes opened wide as she said, "I've always wanted to live in Santa Fe and open a painting studio for my artwork."

"I know. How about coming with me?"

She put her cup down and frowned. "I hate flying in planes. I've never been able to get over it."

"Not even if I am there to protect you?" he said, grinning.

Leann just shook her head and said, "You'll have to make this trip by yourself." Now it was his turn to frown. "Don't be sad. I'll be here when you get back, and I'll even mow your lawn, it needs it, and yes, I'll still go up in a helicopter with you."

"I don't like leaving you alone."

"What could happen?"

"Longtree is out there somewhere," John said, standing and walking over to grab a cup.

Leann slowly shook her head. "He's probably in Canada by now," she said as she turned to watch him. "Anyway, I have to go to my home, check out the damage and call work. Or are you going to be my sugar daddy?" she said, laughing.

John almost choked on his coffee and said, "Not without a job."

"Then go there and show them you're a top-flight helicopter pilot," she said, smiling.

John had to resign himself to the fact he wasn't going to win this discussion. Still, the image of Longtree in the picture chewed at his guts. "Let's finish our coffee and then we can stop at the airport to check on flights before heading to my place," Leann said.

He nodded and thought of Prowler to watch over her and felt a little more at ease. *Maybe I could have Ryan Porter stop and check on Leann from time to time*, he thought. Then he had an even better idea.

29

David Longtree's head tossed from side to side, trapped in a nightmare. As he slept in his rocker, images of Tracy slamming head-first through her windshield to end in a bloody heap once again filled his sleep.

It was Monday morning, one week since her death. As he slept, his rocker felt more like he was strapped in an electric chair, awaiting his own execution. Beads of sweat trickled down his forehead as he mumbled, "No, no, I am innocent."

With a start he awoke to find his hands gripping the armrests in white-knuckle terror. Breathing heavily, he gradually became aware of his surroundings. He found he was in the cabin.

He had not had a decent night's sleep since her death and wondered if he ever would.

As his bloodshot eyes began to focus, he could make out soft rays of orange and yellow sunlight streaming through the windows. He got up to stretch and head to the outhouse to urinate. As his thoughts turned to what may be awaiting him outside, he stopped and turned towards his bed, eyeing his rifle. Maybe the police were already here with the place surrounded and he'd be dying in a hail of gunfire.

"Get a grip on yourself," he told himself as he turned again for the front door. "If I'm to die, let it be today," he said with his right hand on the doorknob.

He took a deep breath and jerked the door open all the way, standing there with his eyes closed. Slowly opening his eyes, he peered out over his lot.

No police. No nothing. Nobody.

He half-smiled and headed over to the outhouse. With the door left wide open, he pulled his jeans down and sat his rump on the cold seat. The musky smell of raw sewage filled his nose as flies buzzed and danced around him.

David finished his business and was about to step out when he heard a vehicle drive up his gravel driveway. Instinct took over as he closed the door and hid inside. "Damn," he said as he thought of his rifle that was out of reach.

Whoever it was, was taking their sweet time. As David looked through the door crack, the beads of sweat returned as he said, "Fucking police bastards." Slowly an old, dark-blue cargo van came into view and parked next to his Explorer. He could not make out who was inside with the tinted windows.

David swatted at the flies that were descending around him. Whoever it was in the van killed the engine. The only sound was the warm wind swaying through the pine trees. He tried to peer closer through the crack in the doorframe and said, "Show yourself, asshole," under his breath.

The driver's side door opened. A man hopped out, looked over at the outhouse, and limped towards the cabin's front door. The man in faded blue jeans and black t-shirt appeared to be in his mid-forties, with grayish-black hair and beard. A large white bandage was over his nose. David searched his memory to put a name to the worn face. He remembered a man with a limp from long ago, but could not place it. Anyway, that man was more than likely dead by now.

Whoever it was made his way to the front door and knocked. He didn't appear to be a threat, so David stepped out and said in a firm voice, "Can I help you?"

The man flinched and turned towards David with a smile and said, "Longtree, I'd recognize you anywhere."

David stopped short and shook his head wildly. It was the man he thought was dead: Todd Rudd.

Todd limped towards him with his right hand extended. "How you been? I haven't seen you in a coon's age."

"Well, if it isn't The Mouse," David said, wondering what he wanted.

Rudd frowned as he shook Longtree's hand. "Don't call me that. I never did like that nickname."

"If you're looking to score some weed, I don't deal anymore. I gave that up years ago," David said.

Todd smiled, reached into his pants pocket, and produced a small, brown, wooden stash case with a brass one-hitter. "I brought my own."

David snorted. "You'll never change. How'd you bang your nose?"

Rudd threw up his arms and shook his head in disgust. "I tried to shake down a helicopter pilot I knew and he got the better of me."

A look of surprise came over David and he asked, "His name John Urbain?"

Rudd filled his one-hitter, offered it to David, and said, "How in the hell did you know that?"

For the first time in a week, David could genuinely smile as he felt his blood pressure drop to near normal. *Exit Chris Fields, enter Todd Rudd.* Already he was thinking how he could manipulate this new pawn.

He accepted Rudd's offer of dope, eyeing him with cold eyes. "Let's talk inside."

As he took a deep hit, he looked over the van and liked what he saw. It could become useful. Todd went on about his exploits in California. David wasn't even listening. His only concern was how to make Urbain pay, and pay bad.

He opened the front door and motioned to Todd to have a seat at the kitchen table. The effects of the dope gripped his mind in euphoric calmness. Yes, Urbain would pay with his life, and he could see it would not take too much prodding to get Todd on board. He sat across from him as his mind ran through the opening gambits of what he wanted to do to Urbain. Maybe a kill shot fast and clean, or maybe an oh-so-slow, painful death. Either way, with Todd's help it could be done. *Yes, a vengeance, a bloody vengeance*, he thought.

"I said, how'd you know it was John Urbain?" Todd asked again, bringing David back into the conversation.

David thought about it and threw caution to the wind. He started from the beginning and told Todd everything that had happened in the last week.

✣ ✣ ✣

A half-hour later, David was done. Todd took a hit and said, "I read about what happened in the *LA Times* and *USA Today*, but I never dreamed it was you behind it all. Fate played a part in this, don't you think? I mean, I was on my way back to Los Angeles when I remembered your cabin up here in the sticks. It's a bitch about your girlfriend. She must have meant a lot to you."

"You'll never know how much, and it's Urbain's fault. He fucked up everything."

"I say it's payback time. We kill him and slip away to LA. You'll like it there. It has everything, and the women are fine," Todd replied.

David smiled and reached over for the one-hitter, taking a long draw. *Or I could kill you here and now, and take your van. The police are not looking for you*, David mused. He put his hands behind his head and rocked his chair back on its back legs. *Nobody could replace Tracy; any fool could fill Chris Fields' shoes*, he thought.

David rocked back and forth, debating if he needed this has-been. Resting the chair on its four legs, he came to a decision that he'd use Todd Rudd for now.

"First, we find out where the prick lives, scope out his pad and wait. Then, when I say so, I'll put his forehead in the crosshairs and take him out." David was filled with the surreal event in slow motion in his mind. He pushed his chair back and went to a pantry drawer, pulling out a phone book.

"Now you're talking. I never did like that creep. He always thought he was better than me." Todd said as he took a hit.

Running a finger down the names of Urbain, he found three listings. The third was for John Daniel Urbain at 2718 West Bonnie Lane in Sun Prairie.

"I know where that is. It's outside of Great Falls," David said, looking over at Todd. "Let's take your van, grab some breakfast, then take a drive." He ripped the page out and stuffed it in his pants pocket.

"Sounds good to me, man. I am hungry. Lead the way," Todd said, standing and running hands through his thinning hair.

David put the phone book away, then took a switchblade from the pantry drawer. He stuffed it into his front pocket without Todd noticing. Todd went out the front door as David said under his breath, "Play it easy, Rudd, or you'll end up in a hole."

30

After breakfast at the same Denny's restaurant, John and Leann drove to the airport. The earliest flight he found was with Southwest Airlines, departing the next day at 7:35 A.M., a nonstop round-trip ticket to Santa Fe. He still felt uneasy leaving Leann by herself. He resigned himself to the fact he needed a job, even if it meant moving there with Leann at his side. Maybe she was right about Longtree leaving Montana.

Possibly he was gone, but leave everything behind? No, it didn't make sense. Maybe he was following them right now, waiting for the right moment to take her out. He checked his mirrors for anything out of the ordinary.

Leann asked, "What's wrong? You seem preoccupied."

Not wanting to fill her with fear, he said, "Nothing. I was just thinking of our anniversary."

With a puzzled look, she asked, "What anniversary?"

"Don't tell me you forgot already. It was one week ago today we met."

"You're right, I almost did forget. My God, so much has happened since then," she said, sliding closer to him and putting her hand on his thigh.

"I don't know what would have happened had you not come along when you did," she said, resting her head on his shoulder. "I was thinking I could call the bank from my home. I am dying to see what my home looks like in the daylight."

"Wherever you want to go," John said.

"Then take a right here and head north on Highway 87."

"I remember how to get there."

"Sorry, I forgot," she said.

"When do you think you'll have to return to work?"

"Well, with the fire, I am sure I can squeeze a few more days, could be a week."

"Make sure you call them. I don't want you to lose your job too," he said, laughing.

One week, it's only been one week. So much has changed, John mused. *Lost my job but gained a girlfriend. Took one man out who tried to hurt her, but one more lurks out there*. He glanced over at her as she took in the countryside. He was glad to have her at his side. He wondered what he liked better: her or flying helicopters. Why not have both?

His mind rolled over to New Mexico. It was time for a change, he was sure of that, and if it made Leann happy, so much the better. He knew he could fly anything that was thrown at him. Yes, a change would do them both good.

They pulled into her driveway. Both could see the home was in need of some repairs. Leann hopped out with her new key, after the insurance company installed a new front door. Brown-black smoke stains were above all her windows. With John beside her, she unlocked the front door and crept inside. The rich smell of burnt wood and plastic permeated their nostrils.

"Let's open all the windows and doors and let the place air out," John said, going throughout the home.

They both walked through the kitchen as John said, "I can fix a lot of this myself, I think."

Leann started to cry as they took in all the damage to the floors and walls. The home had smoke and water damage everywhere. John held her hand as she said, "No, it's better if I just sell the place. I'll never again feel at home here."

"You have a home already," John said as he put his arms around her.

John's mind turned to Longtree. He caused all of this, and he vowed Longtree would pay.

John took Leann by the hands, looking into her damp eyes, and said, "Let's get the hell out of Montana and start a new life somewhere else."

"When you get that Santa Fe opening, that will be our new home," she said, wiping the tears away.

John held her close. "We'll sell our homes and I'll sell my twenty percent ownership at Skyway to Walter Clark. He wants it bad anyway."

"I'm sure I can find a banking job too," she said, now smiling.

"That's my girl. Let's gather your things and then I'll take you out for dinner."

"You're my man," Leann said.

✣ ✣ ✣

One thing was clear to David while Todd drove on to Sun Prairie: He'd have to kill Todd, if for no other reason than just to shut him up.

All through breakfast at a hole-in-the-wall called Lee's Diner on Interstate 15, Rudd ranted on about his trials and tribulations in LA. *What the hell do I care?* He looked over at Rudd and seriously thought of asking him to pull over and garroting him, then dumping his carcass in a ditch. Local and state police rarely patrolled on the side roads by his cabin. He didn't need Rudd, just his van.

As the pot was wearing off, he smiled at the thought of *all in due time*. He needed to be mobile, and with the local and state patrol on the lookout for his Ford Explorer, he didn't have a choice. There was little fear they would see his vehicle at the cabin as he knew they rarely patrolled around there except in the winter months. He planned on being long gone by then.

"Did you hear what I said? LA is the place to score some fine weed, for sure," Todd said, weaving in and out of traffic.

"Slow down, dammit. You want the police on your ass?"

"They're not looking for me, man," Todd said, backing off the gas pedal.

David shot him an angry look and said, "Get in the left lane, Sun Prairie is coming up."

"You decide how you're going to take Urbain out?"

David said, "Between the eyes," checking his mirror for police squads.

"Tell me more about Leann Blake. Is she hot?" Todd wanted to know.

"That bitch should be dead by all rights," David said, slamming his fist against the dash. *Just like Chris Fields, Todd was thinking with his prick first.* "Don't get any ideas. I just want her dead. She's a loose end I want taken care of, that's all."

"That's your score. 'I just want Urbain dead'," Todd mimicked, taking the exit to Sun Prairie.

David directed him to Bonnie Lane on the outskirts of Sun Prairie. He vaguely remembered it being on a cliff road, having made some deliveries from the pawnshop.

"The clouds are turning dark. It looks like rain is heading our way," Todd said, checking the June skyline.

"Just drive on," David said, biting his lower lip in frustration. He checked his watch. It was 9:37 in the morning.

"So what's the plan with this guy?" Todd said, following his directions.

David peered out his window at the first mailbox he saw on Bonnie Lane. They were in the 2500 block. "Okay, slow down a little. It's on my side, up a ways," he said as his heart raced faster. "We're looking for number 2718."

"Got it," Todd said, gently slowing down and scanning the mailboxes on his side.

The asphalt paved road snaked upward gradually. The homes were all two or three hundred feet from the road. "Look at all the land they have up here, rich bastards," David said, scanning the manicured lawns of Sun Prairie.

"This is nothing, you should see LA—"

"Shut up about LA," David said, tapping his fingers in frustration.

At the top of the ridge, David spotted the address. "Stop. Here it is." David looked over the house and yard, thinking only of how best to break in. There was no vehicle in the driveway that ran for a hundred feet off the road.

"Plenty of trees surround his lot. That's good for us," David said, looking at Todd.

The house was towards the top of a ridge, then the road sloped downward. "He's the last house before the road heads down," David said, smiling at Todd. "There's no nosy neighbors to worry about. Drive up a ways and turn around."

Todd put the van in gear and moved on down the road till he was almost at the bottom of the ridge. "Make a U-turn here. We'll park off the road at the bottom of the crest tonight. We'll use the woods surrounding his lot to get into position."

"Then what?" Todd said, turning the van around.

"Then we'll break the back door open, and I'll take him out with one round to his head," David said with wide eyes.

As they passed by the home again, David glanced at the sky that was moving in thick clouds from the west. "A storm is moving in. We go tonight, no matter what. You up for this?" he said, turning towards Todd with a gleam in his eyes.

"Let's do it," Todd said with a smile.

"Head back to my place and we'll catch some sleep. It's going to be a long night. You got any pot left?"

"I thought you'd never ask," Todd said, reaching up to the visor for his one-hitter.

Tonight John Urbain will die by my hands, then the bitch is next, David thought. He took a long hit of pot, then closed his eyes and planned a murder. *Or two.* He opened his eyes and enjoyed the ride.

He looked over at Todd with his bandaged nose and laughed at him.

Man, I'm high.

31

The last rays of twilight cast their long shadows across the wet landscape as the rainstorm moved slowly eastward. John and Leann had spent the better part of Monday cleaning her home the best they could.

"I say we call it a day and get something to eat," John said, wiping sweat from his forehead with a red handkerchief.

Standing next to him in her living room, Leann said, "Sounds good to me," wiping a smudge of dirt from her cheek. He offered his handkerchief but she waved him off. "I just want to take a hot shower and get some food in me," she said, smiling at him.

John toyed with the idea of joining her and running his rough hands over her soft skin, but there was something he needed to do first. "Let's get you squared away at my place. Then I am taking you out for a steak dinner in Great Falls," he said, picking up her suitcase, easel, and art supplies.

"You read my mind like a cheap comic book. I'm in the mood for a good steak about now," she said, opening the front door for him.

The fresh smell of rain filled their nostrils as they loaded her things in the back of his Silverado.

After pulling in his driveway on Bonnie Lane, John got out and was about to open Leann's door when he glanced back towards the road. An old blue cargo van with tinted windows slowly drove by, disappearing over the crest of the hill. Keenly aware of new vehicles in his neighborhood, the hair on the back of his neck started to rise.

"What are you looking at?" Leann asked.

"Nothing." He didn't want to alarm her with Longtree on the loose. He laughed to himself as he looked into her soft eyes. It was probably nothing to worry about.

Just maybe he did leave Montana for good, he pondered.

The sound of Prowler barking in his cage brought John back. He unlocked the front door to his home and said, "Time to feed the master."

"Poor thing," Leann said, stepping inside. "He must be soaked from the rain."

"He loves the rain. He's just glad I'm home. I'll feed him, then I am going for a walk to Ryan Porter's house down the road. I'll be back before you know it. Lock the door."

His only concern was her safety while he was away. Going to Ryan Porter's to borrow a .45 caliber would see to that. "You know how to use a gun?" he asked her, holding her in his arms.

"Sure. My dad taught me when I was little. What's on your mind?"

"You'll see when I get back," he said, kissing her forehead.

✣ ✣ ✣

"That's him," David said as Todd drove by in his van. "His picture was splashed in the newspapers after the bastard saved Blake."

Todd looked over and nodded. "It's show time."

David motioned forward with his right hand. "At the bottom of the hill, pull over and stop."

With a grin on his face, Todd said, "I'm looking forward to this shit."

David reached in the back of the van, grabbed his AK-47 out of its gun case. As Todd parked off the road next to a grove of pine trees, David checked his camouflage pants pockets.

"You got everything?" Todd asked, patting his own .45 caliber in the front of his black jeans.

"Duct tape and this," David said, holding his rifle out, showing Todd.

He turned the engine and headlights off without taking his eyes off the rifle. "My, that's a big one."

David smiled as he got out and put on his black cowboy trench coat. He stowed the rifle inside his jacket, holding it up in his left armpit with his left hand. He leaned in the van and said, "We'll cut through the trees to his house and scope out his lot. Just follow me and keep quiet."

Todd nodded and joined him.

"Let's go," David said, wading into a ditch that ran along the road. Todd followed, almost slipping in the four-inch water. The knee-deep grass and weeds were soaked from the storm.

Reaching the concealment of the pine trees, David motioned with a finger to his lips to be quiet. Once they were out of sight from the road, David took out his rifle and crouched low to avoid the branches. Right on cue, Todd removed his .45, following two steps behind.

David could make out the light from the house a hundred feet ahead of him. The trees were wet and they both made an effort not to bump into them as David went down on one knee.

Reaching into his coat, he produced a six-inch flashlight. Up ahead there was a wall of rocks and boulders three feet high that spanned the length of the lot line. David pointed towards them to Todd, who nodded in agreement. The night was coming on quickly as David turned the flashlight on.

He stood up and half sprinted towards the rock line as Todd followed. Crouching low below the rocks, David waited till Todd was next to him and then peered over the ledge. With the light from the back of the house casting its glow across the backyard, his eyes focused on one object: a caged-in dog patrolling his confinement. David bent down and said, "The bastard's got a dog." He reached into his leg pocket, produced a silencer and screwed it onto his rifle. He looked over at Todd. "Time to put this mutt to sleep, permanently." Todd gave back a puzzled look. "We can't have him barking up a storm, can we?" David said. He adjusted his sight on the dog, which was about 50 feet away in the middle of the yard. He was about to pull the trigger when the back door opened and out walked John Urbain with a dish in each hand.

"Take him out, do it now," Todd said in a low whisper, looking over the crest.

"Get down, you fool," David said, also in a low whisper, not taking his sight off of Urbain.

Todd reluctantly obeyed, throwing up his hands with a *what are you waiting for?* look.

David ignored him, wanting to take him inside his home, for the fringe benefits.

Urbain put the bowls down and unlocked the latch. The dog wanted out. Urbain pushed him back in with his leg. The dog started barking in anticipation of being fed.

"Shut up and eat," they heard Urbain say.

The dog's tail was wagging at a fast clip as he licked his chops and plowed into his bowls. Urbain looked over his backyard and closed the cage door. David watched as he made his way back to the house, leaving the back light on.

"Man, you should have killed him right then and there," Todd said with a look of anguish.

With a free hand, David lunged at Todd, grabbing him by his throat. "I want to look into his eyes and see the fear before I waste him. Do you understand?" He pushed Todd away and said, "We'll do it my way."

Todd rubbed his throat, trying to quell the pain. "Okay, okay, we'll do it your way."

David looked over the ledge and put the crosshairs of the AK-47 on the dog with its head in a bowl. Slowly he squeezed the trigger as a soft, quiet muffle rang out. The dog's head splattered in a rush of pinkish red and he fell over in a heap.

With a grin David chambered the next round, shooting a glance at Todd. "I still got it. One shot, one kill." David couldn't care less; no remorse. He hated dogs.

"Move on down to the front of the house. Let me know if anybody's coming or going. Now we wait for Urbain to settle in. Keep quiet and keep low."

Todd nodded, crouching low. He moved into position behind the rock wall. David nodded to him at his position and waved for him to keep low.

He looked at his watch by the dim porch light and made it at 8:30 P.M. He passed the time eating energy bars that were stuffed in his pants pocket and watched Todd. When he was finished eating, he tossed the wrappers aside and started to doze off.

As sleep was about to overtake him, he awoke to Todd moving towards him. "He's gone. The prick went for a walk down the road," Todd said.

David sprang to his feet and said, "Now we break inside and set a trap for the bastard. Let's go. Hold this," he said to Todd, handing him the AK-47. "We'll break the back door open with this," he said, picking up a loose boulder the size of a softball.

They made their way up and over the rocks towards the back door. "What about an alarm?" Todd asked with a worried look.

David smiled. "That's what the mutt was for."

Todd shot a look back at the cage. "He's not going to bark anytime soon."

David took a firm grip on the boulder and raised it above his head. He brought it down in a swift motion against the brass doorknob three times. The third time the knob gave way and fell to the ground. "We're in," David said as he pushed the door open. "Kill everyone in the house," he added.

He took back his rifle and told Todd to check all the rooms. He took a chair at the kitchen table as Todd disappeared through the living room.

The lights were on in the living room and down the hall. Todd crept back, saying, "Someone's taking a shower. The bedrooms are clear."

"Keep watch at the picture window for Urbain, you idiot. I'll have to handle whoever's in the bathroom myself."

Todd stood his ground, knowing what David had to do.

David stood slowly and came within inches of Todd's face. "Get your ass over to the window and watch for Urbain."

With a lump in his throat, Todd did as he was told.

David walked down the hallway and put his hand to the bathroom door. He heard the sound of a woman humming a song against the backdrop of cascading water. He slowly turned the doorknob and found it to be unlocked. Leaning his rifle against the wall, he grinned and with a push against the door, barged in.

32

As David Longtree burst through the door, he was met with a wave of heat and humidity. He stood there, listening to the woman sing. In an alluring voice she said, "Changed your mind, did you now? Well, come on in and join me."

For the first time since Tracy Burke's death, he wanted a woman sexually. He felt his loins tightening to arousal. The thought of rape crossed his mind.

In a fit of rage, he drew back the curtain. His eyes grew wide.

It was her, Leann Blake, standing naked before him. Before she could scream, he forced his right hand over her mouth as his left hand went around her waist. He pulled her close as he lifted her out of the shower. Their eyes met as he pinned her against the wall. "Remember me?" he said.

Leann's arms were thrashing wildly, knocking a picture off the wall. Leann struggled, trying to kick him in the groin, to no avail.

David clasped his hand tighter over her mouth, yelling for Todd. "Look what I found!"

Todd rushed to the bathroom as David said, without taking his cold eyes off her, "Get the van while I tape her up."

Todd just stood there, leering at her from head to foot.

"Get the van now!" David barked.

Todd sprang into action, saying, "I'm going to nibble on her nougat."

David forced her over to the towel rack, fumbling for a washcloth. In a blink he pulled her wet dark hair violently saying, "So you want to play?"

As she tried again to scream, he stuffed the wash cloth in her mouth. She tried to spit it out as he threw her to the floor. With lightning speed he produced a roll of duct tape and clamped a four-inch strip over her mouth, securing the wash cloth. Flipping her over, he taped her hands behind her back. For the first time in a week, he felt in control. Grabbing her by her taped hands, he lifted her to her feet.

"You're coming with us. Don't try to struggle free, got it?" he said, pulling her head back by her hair. "Do you understand?"

With tears streaming down her face, she nodded.

He smiled, pushing her into the hallway. With one hand around her waist, he grabbed his rifle, pushing her into the living room. Leann fell to her knees as Todd came in the front door out of breath. "Open the back door to the van," David said.

Smiling in lurid anticipation, Todd bolted back out.

David slapped Leann across her mouth, saying, "On your feet, bitch."

Leann rose to her feet as he said, "We're going for a little ride before your boyfriend gets back."

His mind was overcome with the dark thoughts of what he was going to do. He would also let Todd have his way with her as a reward. He had no problem killing her, dumping her body in a shallow grave in some secluded forest upstate. First, he had to get her in the van and be gone before her boyfriend returned. He smiled at the thought of taking a picture of her tied up and sending it to Urbain.

It was dark outside as he pushed her to the van. Todd was standing by with the back doors open, playing lookout.

Yes, David grinned as he thought of Urbain wondering what had happened to his beloved. After the deed was done, maybe he would take up Todd's offer and split to California.

Todd rushed over to him and lifted Leann's legs as he came

down the front steps. “After we get her in, you drive,” he said to a grinning Todd.

“Where we taking her?”

“To the cabin so we can have some fun,” David said, laughing.

“Sounds good to me.”

33

John Urbain found himself looking down at his work boots as he walked from Ryan Porter's home. The air was cool and calm. The only sounds were the nighttime insects. As he looked up, he caught the smell of himself and knew he needed a shower. He didn't really want to go out to dinner. Just a quiet night at home with Leann was what he craved.

Maybe the worst was over, John thought. It just might be that Longtree had split town, if not the state. He'd leave it to the police to solve. Still, he felt better knowing that in his left hand he carried a blue gym bag with a snub-nosed .38 tucked away. Loaded and ready, its six shots could bring down any man, even Longtree. With that and the sure eyes of Prowler he felt Leann would be secure while he was away. He wondered if asking the police for a female officer to stay with Leann was too much. He would ask Detective Lewis for more patrols in the neighborhood.

A gentle breeze stirred as the edge of his driveway came into view, blocked only by his neighbor's huge willow tree with its branches almost touching the ground.

Then his blood ran cold.

A blue van with tinted windows was backed up in his driveway.

To make matters worse, there was the unmistakable Todd Rudd with an unknown man, who he guessed was David Longtree, tossing a naked Leann into the back of the van!

John's instincts took over. He ran behind the willow tree for protection as his body burst out in a cold sweat. He crouched behind the willow trunk as his hands fumbled into the gym bag for the loaded .38. *It ends here and now*, he thought. *Give me one clean shot*.

Now spread-eagled flat on the damp ground, he peered from behind the tree trunk, breathing hard. Todd was sprinting towards the driver's door. John took careful aim with the snub-nose's tritium night sight, drawing a bead on Todd's chest. He guessed the distance at 25 yards as he yelled, "Hey asshole!" to Rudd.

Todd looked stunned as he turned towards the voice, drawing his Colt .45 from behind him in one smooth motion. He took a firing stance and yelled, "It's him!" while squeezing off three rounds.

John ducked behind the willow as shards of bark exploded around him. He gripped the .38 with both hands. *Only have six rounds*, he had to make them count. In his mind he pictured the crosshairs squarely on Todd's chest. Holding the revolver tightly, he again peered around the tree trunk. Todd was turned away, frantically trying to open the driver side door.

Bracing himself, John took careful aim at the middle of Todd's back. Todd turned and was about to fire as John gently pulled the trigger. The first round was wide, hitting the door. The next round found its mark, hitting Rudd in the chest, throwing him flat against the van. Todd contorted forward, dropping his gun and clutching his chest. He looked upward, falling to his knees as blood poured from his wound. He staggered forward and crumpled to the ground, landing on his face in the driveway.

"One down, one to go," John said as he looked for the other man. He was about to move from behind the tree trunk. By his porch light, he could make out the ponytailed man lurking behind the van. Even at that distance John could see the silver and black AK-47 Kalashnikov the man was holding.

"Oh, shit," John said as he tried to make himself smaller behind the tree.

In an instant the rapid fire of rounds strafed the trunk and surrounding grass. John tried in vain to think of how many rounds an AK-47 held. One thing was certain: it was more than he had left.

If the man continued to advance, John was at his mercy. His only hope was a quick discharge of remaining rounds from his .38. *Easy now, John*, he said to himself.

Taking a deep breath, he summoned all his willpower and quickly looked around the tree. It had to be the owner of the pawnshop. He yelled, "Hey Longtree, you'll never leave my driveway alive!"

The man was on one knee, bending over Todd. He was taking what appeared to be Todd's wallet. John hoped someone had the forethought to call the police. If he could only keep him talking…

"Don't bet on it," Longtree yelled back, now standing, spraying fire in John's direction.

"Bastard," John said, trying to squeeze himself behind the tree.

John was about to return fire when the thought of Leann getting hit with a stray shot popped into his head. He heard the van door slam and peeked around to see the man in the front seat, starting the engine. John stood from behind the tree taking careful aim. *It's now or never*, he thought with four rounds left.

He shot two rounds at the man's head as the van lurched forward, both missing their mark. The van quickly turned north as he tried a shot at the back tires, praying he did not harm Leann.

"Not so fast, asshole," John said, running towards his pick-up to give chase. He spit on Todd as he ran by him.

The sound of the van heading downhill died away. John looked up. Longtree had shot out both back tires of his pick-up.

He was alone. Leann was taken from him.

He felt blood on his hands as he ripped his t-shirt off to see his stitches had come undone. John looked back at Rudd's lifeless body. Their eyes met—one's heart still beating, the other turning cold as the wind picked up.

The van and Leann were long gone as John sank down in the damp grass of his front yard. For the first time in years, his eyes welled up with tears. He cried as he heard sirens in the far distance. They were too late to save her. John failed to protect her.

He vowed to get her back no matter the cost. He was not going to lose Leann.

34

As the sirens drew closer, John Urbain could see the cascading red and blue lights reflecting off his neighbor's windows, the wet pavement, and driveways like the dance floor of a disco club.

He didn't want to be seen standing there with a .357 Magnum in his hands. So he laid it down and put his hands in the air. The last thing he needed was law enforcement thinking he was the prime shooter.

Two police cruisers converged from opposite directions to form a wedge in front of his lot. One by one nosy neighbors opened their front doors or drew their curtains back to look.

With weapons drawn, both officers took a defensive position behind their vehicles, aiming their squad-mounted spotlights on John. "You there, hands up and hit the ground now!" a female officer shouted.

John sprawled out in a spread-eagle position on the wet grass of his front lawn. Keeping his mouth shut for the time being, his thoughts were on Leann and Longtree getting further and further away. He closed his eyes, waiting for the inevitable handcuffs. He grunted as he felt a knee clamp down on the back of his neck, pressing his face into the damp sod. His hands were forcefully placed behind his back and in cuffs in a flash.

"My name is John Urbain, I live here. There's been a kidnapping and they're getting away," he said, trying to remain calm.

The officers lifted him to his feet, causing John to cry out in pain due to his shoulder. "Tell it to the detective," the female officer said as he was hurried to one of the squads.

The deafening sound of more squads could be heard approaching from, what seemed to John, every direction. The female officer held him by his cuffs as the other placed a hand on John's head, opened the back door of the squad, and tossed him in.

"His name is David Long…" was all John could say before the door was slammed shut. His mind filled with anger at how long it would take till somebody would listen. His left shoulder throbbed as he twisted his arms, trying to make himself comfortable. Giving in to his predicament, he relaxed the best he could and leaned his head back on the seat.

John could only shake his head at the thought of Leann and what she must be going through. He spent the next couple of minutes taking deep breaths to calm himself and his mind. Every direction he looked there were flashing lights reflecting off the squads, homes, pavement, and the body of Todd Rudd.

Two officers were standing over Rudd taking notes. John counted six officers running around. One cordoned off a wide area of the crime scene with yellow DO NOT CROSS tape.

Out of the corner of his eye, he spotted an unmarked car making its way through the tangle of squads. "Thank God," he said as he recognized Detective James Silva emerge and take charge. John had met him at a search-and-rescue class a few months back as Det. Silva gave a lecture on emergency first aid. At 6'2" with brown-gray eyes, he looked more like General Patton barking orders than an 18-year veteran of the Great Falls police force.

A junior officer ran up to him pointing in John's direction. Det. Silva nodded and walked over to John's squad. Opening the door, he was surprised to see John Urbain in cuffs. "You've got to be kidding me. John, is that you?" he said with a grin.

"It's me…again."

"You just can't seem to stay out of trouble, can you? What happened here?"

John spent the next 20 minutes giving the sordid details of Longtree, Rudd, and Blake and their relationship together, starting with the ambush.

"And you say it was a blue van with tinted windows?" Det. Silva asked.

"Positive," John replied.

"I'll be back in a few. I'll call this in as an all-points bulletin. If we're lucky, state patrol will intercept Longtree," Det. Silva said.

John could only watch helplessly as his neighbors came within the limits of the DO NOT CROSS tape.

His next-door neighbor, a crusty old man, shouted out, "You're paying for that willow tree and grass."

Others joined in. "It's time you moved. This used to be a quiet suburb."

"I hope they lock him up." someone shouted.

John shook his head in dissatisfaction, shouting back, "Go to hell, all of you."

"Don't bother with them," Det. Silva said, returning. "I've got some bad news for you," he continued. John feared the worst: that they had found Leann's naked body by some roadside. "Your dog is dead and your back door looks as if that's where they broke in."

"Bastards," John said with a grimace. "Any word on Leann?" he continued, his eyes growing moist.

"Nothing yet. Don't worry, she'll turn up," Det. Silva said, instantly regretting he'd said it. "I mean alive," correcting himself, and added, "Let me get those cuffs off you."

"Thanks. I can't wait to get my hands on Longtree. I am going to wring that ponytailed bastard's neck," John growled.

"I've put a call in to the FBI because of the kidnapping, plus the state police. Just let us handle it."

Wiping the tears from his face, John looked up at Det. Silva and choked, "Get her back alive. I love her."

Det. Silva put his hand on John's shoulder. "We will."

35

"Damn prick," David Longtree said as he slipped in and out of traffic, putting as much distance between himself, Urbain, and the police as possible. He needed time to think. Heading west down I-15 to his cabin at Holter Lake, still a few miles from the Wolf Creek exit, images came flooding in waves: Tracy Burke, Lamar Singleton, Gregory Cameron, Chris Fields, and now Todd Rudd, all dead.

Soaked in sweat, he wiped snot from his nose as he checked the time—12:06 A.M., Tuesday, a new day. He wondered if it was to be his last.

In his overhead rearview mirror he caught Leann Blake struggling under a dirty gray blanket. What's one more killing? Kill her, head to the cabin, regroup, and try to make it to Canada before morning. His queen was dead and he'd lost all of his pawns. Now he had Urbain's queen laid out before him.

With the whole police force of Montana looking for him, he knew his odds of escape were slim at best.

Traffic was light as he turned off the Wolf Creek exit, turning left down Recreation Road. He looked over at his AK-47 lying on the seat next to him. "There's no way I'm going to prison," he said, checking his mirrors for the law.

Oncoming headlights flashed in his eyes from the steep grade up ahead. David stiffened in his seat as the out-of-state station wagon passed by. "I'm not going to live like this," he said.

He thought of his brother Carl rotting in prison in Wisconsin. "No way," he barked.

He heard thunder in the distance and light rain peppered his windshield. Todd's police scanner came to life. "This is an all-points bulletin. Be on the lookout for a dark-blue, late-model van with tinted windows, wanted in connection with a kidnapping of one Leann Blake. Suspect is armed and dangerous," the officer said.

Upon hearing her name, Leann tried to scream but couldn't with the duct tape over her mouth. It was all she could do to breathe.

"Nobody can save your ass now. Let the police look all they want," David said. "Well, it's time we end this game," he continued. *Dump her now, I've got nothing more to lose.*

He passed by a green-and-white highway sign that said *Missouri River Crossing Ahead.* He saw his opportunity.

There was a wide bridge span with no traffic around.

The road was empty as he pulled over and stopped in the center of the bridge span. Leaving the engine running, he leaped out and opened the back doors. Having gone over this bridge countless times, he knew it was a good 40 feet down to the rushing waters, a deep limestone gorge lined the side walls with jagged boulders.

He reached in and ripped the blanket from her. David looked into her eyes that were wide with fright. Sullen, empty of feelings about what he planned to do made him smile as he glossed over the length of her naked, slender body. "If I only had more time," he said as he closed his eyes and lifted her up and out. All he could hear was Leann's muted screams and the rushing water in his ears. David knew he would hear her screams in his nightmares for the rest of his life.

In the pitch-darkness he heard the rumble of thunder in the distance as rain pelted his face. He carried her over to the metal guardrail.

He opened his eyes and took one last look at Leann. He had no words to say. Naked, bound, gagged, she was heaved over the side. He heard her hit the water and rocks below.

He quickly slammed the back doors and hopped into the driver's seat. Wiping the rain from his face, he fled the scene.

For the second time in one week—one by proxy, he committed murder.

David felt nothing.

No remorse.

Nothing.

36

In the light rain, Detective Silva stood over the body. "Who's the dead guy?" he asked John Urbain without looking up.

John observed the crumpled body silently for a moment before answering him. "This piece of human waste is Todd Rudd. I knew him in the Air Force a long time ago, he's a bum."

Det. Silva wrote the name down in a small brown notebook, trying his best to shield it from the rain.

"The more we stand around here, the farther they get. You should be running down Longtree, who kidnapped Leann," John said.

"We're doing everything we can," Det. Silva said. "Take it easy," he added.

Moving to within inches of the detective's face, John said, "Don't tell me to take it easy. He's got Leann!"

The detective stood his ground, glancing up at the rainstorm. "Let's go inside and finish this."

"Sure let's give him all the time he needs with my naked girlfriend."

John shook his head, walking away. He stopped to kick Rudd in the stomach, saying, "No, let's get this over with now. I'll look for her myself."

With a snort, Det. Silva pointed his pen over his left shoulder without turning around and said, "Not in that truck you're not."

John spun around, looking back at his Silverado with the blown-out tires. "Shit," John said, folding his hands behind his head. He took a deep breath, regaining some control. "I'm sorry. I just want Leann back. Let's get out of the rain," he said, walking towards his truck to retrieve his garage door opener.

Det. Silva followed two steps behind, saying, "John, I've got a photo for you to look at."

Stepping into the garage, John asked, "Of what?"

Det. Silva reached inside his dark blue sports jacket for a handkerchief and a photo. "It's a Department of Motor Vehicles photo of David Longtree." John froze. "Is this the man you saw tonight with Mr. Rudd?" handing both items to John.

John ignored the handkerchief and took the photocopy. John walked over to his work bench to turn on the overhead light. He sat on a stool, peering into the cold, dark-brown eyes of Longtree, quickly handing it back. "It's him, all right." Det. Silva stuffed the picture in his jacket. "Leann told me she accidentally went to his pawnshop, not knowing he planned the ambush. Then the bastard tries to kill her with fucking bees."

Det. Silva nodded. "Plus that's where Det. Lewis was stabbed. I read the reports."

"And I killed Fields before he could finish the job," John added.

"No argument there. Thank you, he's a good man. We've put two patrolmen on a twenty-four-hour stake-out on the pawnshop, but so far no luck."

Over Det. Silva's shoulder, John could make out a long white station wagon turning into his driveway. "The meat wagon's here for that piece of shit Rudd."

"Any idea on how Rudd knew Longtree?" Det. Silva asked, stuffing his notebook in his breast pocket.

"Beats me," John said, shaking his head.

Det. Silva looked at his wristwatch. "It's after midnight and I need to get back to the station. I'll let you know if I hear anything. Also I'll have more information in the morning."

"Find her," John said, rising from his stool.

"You have the Great Falls police, state patrol, and the FBI all doing their best. Hang in there and try to get some rest."

John stood there watching the detective take four steps into the rain, only to stop, turn around, and say with a smile, "Oh, and don't do anything stupid, okay? I'll catch you in the morning."

Smiling, John gave him a thumbs-up sign, only to give him the middle finger when he turned his back.

✣ ✣ ✣

John sat on his porch in the rain, soaked to the bone, watching as the police finished their investigation. Nobody said anything to him, much less even looked at him.

He had to smile as the morgue personnel loaded Rudd into the back of the white station wagon. "Bastard. Rot in hell," he said. A burly man in a gray jumpsuit slammed the back door to the wagon.

He hung his head, thinking of what Rudd would have done to Leann. A slow rape tied up, and then what? He pictured Longtree laughing throughout. Looking up into the falling rain, he said, "Leann, where are you?"

What will Longtree do to her?

Mild shock set in and he knew.

John checked his watch: it read 1:13 A.M. Tuesday. He stood slowly; his mind turned over the task at hand. He had to cover Prowler for the night. He would lay him to rest in the morning. He retrieved a flashlight and blanket from his truck, making his way towards the back of his home.

He stopped and shook his head at the sight of his back door hanging by one hinge, swaying in the cool breeze.

Next was Prowler's cage. His flashlight found his dog with its head almost completely blown away. Bits of brain matter were sprayed on the doghouse and hanging by a thread on the cage. John opened the cage, remembering the good times they enjoyed duck hunting together. *Fucking sadistic bastard*, he thought, spreading the blanket. "Rest in peace, my friend."

His hands clenched in rage as he walked up to his garage. He needed a killing tool for protection, as the police had confiscated his friend's revolver. What was he supposed to do if Longtree came hunting him? On his back wall he found a three-foot-long machete. "This will have to do for now." The machete felt good in his hands, slashing back and forth. "One chance, Longtree, that's all I'll need," he vowed.

✣ ✣ ✣

John stripped down, changing into a dry t-shirt and shorts. The ripped stitches were starting to scab over and only required a quick wash and a bandage. *Now for a stiff drink*, he thought. Reaching into his liquor cabinet above his stove, he found what he was looking for: a half-filled bottle of bourbon. He noticed his hands were shaking as he took two long pulls from the bottle. Shuffling into his living room with the bottle in one hand and the machete in the other, he slumped into his recliner.

His mind raced with possibilities, none of them good for Leann. He laid the machete across his lap and took another pull. He wiped his mouth as the bourbon took hold of him. He let out a deep sigh and closed his eyes. Running the events of the past week was like shuffling a deck of cards in his mind:

The ambush
Seeing Leann
Meeting her in the hospital
Losing my job
The bees
The house fire
Killing Chris Fields
Losing Prowler
Her warm body next to me
Her deep bluish-green eyes
And future possibilities

He was numb, not only from the bourbon. He had known her only one week…*and now she's gone. Where is she?*

Gripping the machete, he slowly fell asleep with images of Longtree and vengeance playing in his mind.

37

David Longtree turned sharply off the road onto his long gravel cul-de-sac driveway. Dodging potholes, he had only 100 more yards to his sanctuary. He'd removed his trench coat down to his black t-shirt and blue jeans, now soaked from rain and sweat. Killing was easy. Living with it was the hard part.

The rain had stopped but he still saw flashes of lightning to the east. Breathing the cool night air through his nostrils brought relief that amazed him. He knew he should feel remorse, but there was none. He smiled at the thought of killing her after midnight by throwing her off the bridge.

As his headlights came upon his Ford Explorer, he slowed to a crawl. Gripping the stock of the AK-47 with one hand, he was ready for a fight. His mind turned over the possibility of law enforcement concealed among the pine and spruce trees, waiting to pounce. They seemed to be dancing, like ghosts in the fog of his mind. *Paranoia is settling in for the long haul*, he thought.

David pulled alongside his truck, shutting the engine off and scanning for movement in the darkness. *Maybe they're behind the trees or already in my cabin*, he wondered.

He saw what he thought was a muzzle flash. A few seconds passed and he realized it was only the distant lightning. The night was filled with the shrill chirping of crickets after the storm.

He switched on the dome light and Rudd's police scanner. There was no new information on him. Checking his watch, he read 1:35 A.M. Tuesday.

David leaned back in his seat, taking a deep breath, letting his heart rate return to normal.

Closing his eyes, he saw his stern gray-haired mother in a drunken stupor when he was only eight saying, "Your eyes, those black holes from hell. You'll probably end up a murderer like your father."

He gripped the steering wheel tightly, opening his eyes to his own reflection in the rearview mirror. "You were right, Ma, you bitch."

He turned the light off and took a moment to listen to the scanner for updates. Nothing new. David got out of Rudd's van with the AK-47 in one hand and flashlight in the other. He made his way slowly to the back door.

Then he saw it: a note was taped to the door of the cabin. He read it aloud: 'Sorry I missed you. Rent due today. Will stop by at nine o'-clock tomorrow. Have the cash. Billy Ridge'.

David laughed, looking at Rudd's van and finding his own truck, now both worthless with the police searching for them. There was no way he could escape from Montana in them. The only question was how to kill Ridge and take his vehicle.

David stepped slowly into his cabin grinning, already formulating a plan in his mind.

38

"Help me, John, save me!"

He awoke from the nightmare with a start, the voice of Leann screaming in his mind. Still in the recliner, his mouth was dry and he smelled of sweat. His watch read 8:30 A.M. John's bloodshot eyes came into focus, slowly scanning his living room, then out the picture window. There was police tape strewn here and there throughout his yard. The sunlight outside was obscured by low-hanging gray clouds. The fog was rolling in like tentacles of death.

He felt a chill in his bones as he got up, almost falling down. Then it hit him—a massive hangover. The bottle of bourbon was down to one shot remaining. He grabbed the bottle and the machete and staggered into the kitchen for a much-needed black coffee with the last of the bourbon.

As John waited for the coffee to brew, he remembered where he was to be today: stepping off a plane in Santa Fe, New Mexico for his interview. "Fucking Longtree," he said. All he could do was call and explain the situation to Robert Tyre. He found his cell phone on the counter and called. He could feel his heart race. He wanted this job; he needed it.

He left a detailed message on Tyre's voicemail. "Probably never hear back from him," he said, feeling low and lost. All he could think about was Leann and with each passing hour it seemed more hopeless. He was sure he would need a miracle.

He downed a full cup of coffee heading to the bathroom to check out the damage. John felt older than his 42 years. His muscles and body ached. His wound was healing slowly; it was tender to the touch.

Running his hands through his black hair, he was taken aback by how gray it seemed in one week. "My God, it's only been a week," he muttered. John felt his life spinning like rotor blades, too fast and out of control. Was it his fate to lose her like this? he wondered, *One week to meet her, to love her, and lose her?*

"Focus, dammit," he said into his reflection in the mirror.

John kept his cell phone close just in case Detective James Silva called with any news. His mind turned over and over with Leann like a caged cougar.

He stripped down, showered, and shaved as quickly as he could. He went into his bedroom; the soft scent of her perfume nearly floored him. He sat at the end of his bed and put his head in his hands. Tears welled up, thinking of her smile. He knew he had to get out of the house and do something. *Anything.*

He dressed as fast as he could in a Skyway Tours t-shirt and faded blue jeans with cowboy boots. "Fuck 'em," he said as he strode out the front door, first to put his spare on his Silverado, *I'll have to limp it to the station to get this other one repaired,* then to lay Prowler to rest. After that...what? Maybe take a ride to Silva's office for any news.

John found it hard to focus on putting the spare on without worrying about Leann. As he finished, his cell phone went off. Almost afraid to answer it, he let it ring four times before he said, "Hello?"

"What the hell happened last night? I heard gunshots and police—" It was Ryan Porter.

"He took her, I got one of them, but he took her from me," John said, barely able to contain himself. He spent the next 20 minutes reliving it in slow motion in his mind. Having to explain who Longtree was gave him a throbbing headache. "Look, maybe I'll stop over later, but I still have to bury my dog and then I've just got to get out of here for a while," John said, wondering if aspirin would do the trick.

"Sure thing, John. If I can help in any way, let me know. I just can't believe it," Ryan said.

"Thanks, Ryan. I'll keep that in mind. Come to think of it, I need a spare. Can I borrow yours?"

"Yeah, I'll drive it over to you. Where's the gun you borrowed last night?"

John didn't answer that question. "Just hurry! When I find him, I'm going to kill him," The rising sun had quickly burned the fog away and the clouds had moved on. The Montana sky was turning bright blue, in contrast to his mood.

He took his spade and dug next to an old knotty pine on the back of his lot where Prowler used to play. With each shovelful, John grew more restless, and he wondered if Longtree would come hunting him.

At first he thought his mind was playing tricks on him—the faint sound of rotor blades drawing closer. John stopped digging as he stood still listening. Looking up, he saw a flash of it between the branches. One of Skyways' Bell 206L LongRangers, more than likely with that prick Walter Clark at the controls. John imagined Walter laughing at the thought of him being terminated as the helicopter banked away to the south.

Gripping the spade, he noticed his knuckles were turning white from anger. "All in due time," he said, resuming his chore.

✣ ✣ ✣

As Prowler was laid to rest, John put the finishing touches on the mound. He stood up, straightening his back, wiping the sweat from his brow. With his back to the house, he was sure he sensed someone was walking towards him; more like creeping towards him. Could it be Longtree? He dared not turn around, but planted his feet firmly. He waited till the person was within range before tightening his grip and swinging his spade with all his strength at the person behind him.

39

For Homicide Detective James Silva, this was the part of the job he regretted the most. How do you tell somebody a loved one is dead, murdered in the prime of life? *And where in the hell is Longtree?* Leaving the crime scene miles behind him, the images of Leann's body haunted him. Having seen some murders in his time, being bound, gagged, and thrown off a bridge naked was a new spin.

Seeing Urbain's truck in the driveway, he waved at the man putting on a spare and composed himself before knocking on the front door. With no answer, he went around the garage and saw John burying his dog.

Let's get this over with, he said to himself as he drew closer with John's back to him.

"Good mor…" was all he could say as the arc of a spade missed his throat by inches. Falling backward, he pulled his .357 Magnum, shouting, "Drop it now or you're dead!" Urbain dropped the spade, looking down the barrel of a very nasty weapon.

"Oh, man. I'm sorry. I thought you were Longtree. Let me help you up," he said, extending his right hand.

Det. Silva sat there deciding if he should accept the offer. Finally, extending his left hand, Urbain pulled him to his feet. He holstered his Magnum.

"Do you know how close you came to ending up in the morgue? Not to mention all the paperwork you'd cause me," the detective said with a scowl.

"I am sorry. I'm just—"

"You're worried about Miss Blake, which I can understand." At this moment he felt he was nothing more than a messenger of death.

He gestured for Urbain to have a seat in a nearby lawn chair. Det. Silva reached into his tan sport coat for a smoke, frowning when he saw he had only one left.

"I am here to fill you in if you're up to it," he said, lighting the cigarette.

"Did you find her?" John said, his eyes growing moist.

"There's no easy way to say this. We found her." Det. Silva took a step forward to place a hand on John's shoulder to help expel the shock that was sure to come. "She was found at six-fifteen this morning by two fisherman up by Holter Dam in the Missouri River. I am sorry, but she's dead."

"Are you sure it's her?" John said, burying his head in his hands, starting to cry.

"It's her." He continued, "How much do you want to know?"

"Everything," John said with his head still down.

Det. Silva took a long hit, then flicked the half-smoked butt in the grass. "After she was found, they happened to flag down a state patrol car that was cruising the area. I got the call soon after and went there straight away to head the investigation. I am taking over for Detective Dana Lewis, who's still in the hospital."

John looked up into the detective's eyes, asking, "Was she raped?"

"We won't know till an autopsy is performed. I am sorry." Det. Silva debated on how much he should disclose to John. *Why cause undue grief?* he thought.

"How did she die?" John asked, wiping tears from his eyes.

Det. Silva said, "It appears she suffered blunt force trauma to the head, but again, we won't know till…"

"—an autopsy is performed," John said, finishing the sentence. To Det. Silva, John appeared to be staring off in the distance, trying to comprehend her death.

"What's being done to find Longtree?" John asked, trying to stand.

"Easy now," Det. Silva said, gently holding him down. "I'll have to notify her parents. Did she mention them?" he asked, trying to evade the question about Longtree.

"They live in Casper, Wyoming," John said, growing impatient.

"I'll find them," Det. Silva said, dying for another smoke. He felt for him. No matter how much training he received, he never felt consoling was his strong point.

"Answer me, dammit. Where's Longtree?" John asked.

What can I say? Det. Silva thought. There was no sign of him. No new information. He had to be strong and look John Urbain in the eyes.

"We are doing everything we can to apprehend him. I checked with the Department of Vehicles property tax rolls. No record other than the pawnshop. He has no criminal record I can see. He has an older brother, Carl, doing time in Waupon State Prison in Wisconsin, but it's unlikely he'll head there. I am still confident we'll catch him. His DMV picture has been given to all the airlines. All major roads out of the state are watched by the state patrol. Our border with Canada has been alerted. Even the bus and train stations are on the lookout. Plus, I have a meeting with the FBI later today." Det. Silva noticed a smile forming on John's face.

"So he's trapped," John said.

"Essentially, yes, and now he's wanted for kidnapping and murder, quite possibly two murders," Det. Silva said, leaning in closer out of sympathy.

"The bank president?" John asked.

"You got it. Gregory Cameron. After I left you yesterday, I went poking around the pawnshop. I found what appeared to be a new hole dug behind a wood shed. I took a chance and, sure enough, it was him. I had the job of telling his wife. No easy task," Det. Silva said, checking his watch.

"So where do we go from here?" John asked.

"We? There is no 'we,' John. Let us handle it," Det. Silva said, starting to get a bad feeling in his gut.

“You expect me to just let it go?” John said, raising his voice.

“Yes, I do. If you impede this case in any way, I’ll arrest you myself,” Det. Silva said sternly.

John, with a smile, said, “Thanks for coming over.”

“Don’t give me that phony smile. I mean it. I’ll arrest you,” Det. Silva said, turning to leave.

As he walked out of earshot, he muttered, “He’s going to be a problem. I can feel it,” under his breath.

He’d seen John’s kind before, always thinking they could outsmart the law. Shaking his head, he said, “Revenge,” as he pulled out of the driveway. He knew he’d have to keep an eye on him. He toyed with the idea of assigning an officer to follow John as he headed to the office.

Yes, I will have to keep an eye on him, he thought.

40

David Longtree was not a man accustomed to waiting around. He glanced at his watch—10:50 A.M. Tuesday. That crusty bastard Billy Ridge was two hours late. Not that David had any intention of paying him his rent anyway. In fact, only one person would leave this place alive, and he planned on it being himself.

He had awakened at 8:00 ready and willing to get the dirty deed over with. He passed the time cleaning his AK-47 and Rudd's Colt .45. Both had nearly full clips ready to go if need be.

He'd gone through his plan of killing Ridge a hundred times in his mind.

Maybe Ridge would be driving his huge brown motor home, like he was fond of doing. Having never married and with few friends, Ridge was a loner. Hell, David remembered, he didn't even read the newspaper, watch TV, or listen to the radio. Billy Ridge was all about making money. He never spent a dime he didn't have to. David smiled. He just needed a little luck to drive his way. His focus was his own survival, with little concern for others.

He was hungry and smelled of sweat, but that could wait. His small refrigerator held only four bottles of spring water, one of which he had for breakfast.

David went through Rudd's wallet he had taken off him as he lay dying yesterday. He found $2,200 in cash, two credit cards, a driver's license with a Los Angeles residence, and the address for the pawnshop. He flicked the license in the garbage and kept the rest. He took out his own wallet and dug out his only picture of him and Tracy Burke. It was of them at Yellowstone last summer, holding hands in the rain. *She was a beautiful lady and I loved her.*

David realized he'd never told her that he loved her. He closed his eyes and shook his head. She had to have known. They did everything together.

He gritted his teeth and wiped tears from his eyes. She was gone forever. The only woman he had ever loved. Now she was a cold corpse.

He neatly put the picture back in his wallet. This was not the time to rehash the past. *Keep your head clear; then try to escape out of Montana,* he thought.

The image of the police closing in brought him back to reality. "Time to listen to the scanner," he said to himself as he stuffed Rudd's .45 in the front of his pants.

David opened the back door to a bright-blue, cloudless sky with the temperature at least in the low seventies—and no police. He ran to Rudd's van and jumped in. He turned on the police scanner and waited. He listened with a single purpose: needing to know what law enforcement was planning. The reception was lousy as he fine-tuned the broadcast. He smiled. There was nothing new, just the odd broadcast of state police bitching about all the out-of-state traffic.

"Where in the hell are you?" he growled, again growing impatient with Ridge not showing up. As he rechecked both outside mirrors, he sat up straight. There was Billy Ridge pulling into his driveway. As luck would have it, he was driving his motor home.

As Billy slowly drove up the potholed driveway, David had to admire him. Billy Ridge was a 65-year-old, self-made man. At 6'2", an ex-ranch hand with strong hands, he was nobody's fool. It was known far and wide not to let Billy get his hands around your throat. Quick as a rattler and just as cunning, he had lost little over the years. Still, with his balding white hair, mustache, goatee, wrinkled face, flannel shirt with suspenders, blue jeans and cowboy boots, he was a man from a bygone era. He was about to become extinct, *the old fuck.*

David grinned. No one would miss him, no one would care. David hopped out of the van and waved at Billy, ready to kill him.

Billy Ridge pulled to a stop behind the van and lumbered out. "Longtree, you young sprout. You have my rent money or are you going to give me some song-and-dance excuse?"

David clenched his fists. "Yeah, I got your money, you old goat."

"Well, let's get to it. I've got places to be."

David was ready to lure him in. "Hey, any chance you could take a quick look under the hood?" pointing to the van. "I'll pay you for your time," he added, knowing Billy would not turn down money.

David saw a slow grin form. "You young dudes don't know jack about nothing, do you? Let me get my toolbox."

"Right." As David opened the hood, he thought, *I'll kill the bastard with his own tools.* He grinned when Billy came around the van with an old, rusted-red toolbox.

"Let's see what you got here."

David made sure to keep Billy's back to him as Billy put the toolbox down. *No one will miss him. I'm doing the world a favor*, he thought.

He eyed his weapon of choice when Billy opened the box: an old, worn, ballpeen hammer.

Billy stood looking over the engine as David maneuvered behind him. He reached down, not taking his eyes off of Ridge, and felt around till he came across the ballpeen hammer.

Billy shook his head. "How many miles you got on this piece of junk?"

"I don't know. What does it matter?" David planted his feet firmly, ready to pound a shot into Billy's skull.

As David took a deep breath, a female voice burst over the scanner. "Be on the lookout for one David Samuel Longtree, wanted for murder in…"

"What the hell did you…" Billy said, turning to see a hammer slam into his forehead, caving in his face.

"Die, you old fuck."

Billy wilted to the ground and lay still. There was no need for another blow. David could see blood pouring out of Billy's eyes, ears, and mouth.

David felt nauseated at the sight of so much blood. He could feel the dry heaves that turned into a full-blown vomit as he hunched forward.

He wiped the vomit residue from his mouth and threw the hammer behind the tree line. He broke out in a cold sweat as he dragged Billy's lifeless body and tossed him in the back of the van.

Taking Billy's thick billfold, he slammed the doors, saying, "Rot in hell."

✣ ✣ ✣

After checking out the inside of the motor home, he was relieved to find it had almost a full gas tank, plus some canned goods. Now he could take a warm shower and think on the next course of action. Two murders in two days; but he was too tired to dwell on it. "Fuck 'em," he said.

He looked at his watch. It was almost noon, too late to move today. *Better to hit the highway in the nighttime; fewer police to deal with*, he thought. David looked up. The sky was cloudless but cool for June. "Silent as a mortuary," he said to himself.

He felt sick inside as he made his way to his cabin with warm blood on his hands. He slammed the door behind him. David found it hard to put one foot in front of the other. He was overcome with sleep.

He fell on his bed and melted into oblivion.

41

John Urbain awoke Tuesday afternoon to sunlight in his eyes and ringing in his ears.

After he rubbed his eyes, he realized the noise was only his kitchen phone, louder than he remembered. Blurry-eyed, he checked his alarm clock—2:20 P.M. He had slept longer than he wanted to.

Questions he had no answers for flooded his mind. *How? Why did Leann have to die? Where is Longtree? Is he even in Montana?*

John groaned, rolled over, and covered his ears with his pillow like a sandwich. Unable to dull the noise, he threw his pillow across the bedroom, knocking a framed picture of himself and Leann off his dresser. The piercing crash of glass breaking was a nail to his now throbbing headache.

Dressed only in faded blue jeans, he leaped to his bare feet, almost falling over. "Damn it," he yelled as he saw what he had done to the picture. It was a picture of them after the press conference.

He dodged shards of glass now embedded in his plush, dark-blue carpet, making his way to the hallway. He had to place his hands on both walls for support.

On what seemed like its twentieth ring, he grabbed the receiver and let it drop to dangle inches from the floor. A wave of dizziness overcame him as he stood weak-kneed, trying to shake the cobwebs clear. *Why am I in bed in the afternoon anyway?* he thought.

He knew why: Leann's death and the unavoidable aftermath to follow.

His mouth was dry as he licked his lips in search of cold water and whiskey. John snatched a whiskey bottle off his kitchen table and took a long, hard pull. He made his way to the faucet and drank his fill, splashing his face to no avail. John felt dry and used up.

He stood there, trying to comprehend what to do next. John didn't know whether to laugh or cry. *Leann was taken from me; no job; Longtree is on the loose. Even Prowler is dead.*

He took the whiskey bottle in his hand and thought of Leann. "I'm turning into a drunken bum." John was sweaty, unshaven; his breath smelled of stale alcohol. He could not remember the last time he had felt so low.

With a deep breath, he poured the last of the whiskey down the drain. "I'm a lot of things, but I am not a drunk," he muttered, splashing his face once more with cold water. John didn't even bother to towel down, letting the cool droplets cascade down his naked chest.

He picked up the receiver and listened to only a dial tone. He placed it down on the counter. He was in no mood to talk right now anyway. His headache was pounding with every breath he took.

As he headed back to his bedroom, there was a loud knock at his front door. "Now what? Who in the hell could that be?" he said with a sigh. With an uneven balance, John entered his living room to peek out his picture window with the drapes drawn.

There was another knock, followed by a firm male voice. "Come on, Urbain. We know you're in there. You took the phone off the hook." Then another knock, even louder.

Slowly John moved the drapes to see who the hell it was. Then he caught sight of them: four or more what appeared to be reporters milling around on his stoop. "Oh shit, I don't need this right now," he said, his anger growing. The damn police must have leaked the story of Leann's death, he reasoned, or maybe it was the FBI. Sure as hell somebody did. "Why come to me?" he said aloud.

John took another deep breath and opened the door. "What the hell do you want? I've got nothing to say. No comment." Before they could say a word, John noticed the reporters were taken aback by his appearance. In the distance he saw two camera crews sprinting up his driveway and two TV vans with satellite feeds parked on the road. Some neighbors were gathered on the street.

John spotted Ryan Porter in the crowd and waved him in. All the reporters turned to Ryan as John stepped aside to let him in. Ryan said over his shoulder, "Leave him alone."

One of the reporters asked, "Is he your lawyer?" as they inched closer.

With a stern look John shot back, "Why would I need a lawyer?"

A barrage of questions started with microphones in his face, the film crews were rolling. A sharply dressed man with slicked-back hair in his early forties stepped forward. "Do you know Miss Blake is dead, murdered up by Holter Dam?"

John closed his eyes. "Yes."

A small woman in a gray pants suit, wearing too much perfume, put her microphone in his face, asking, "Were you two going together?"

"I'd only known her for a week, but I suppose you could say that."

John brushed the microphone away as the sharply-dressed man asked impatiently, "What are you going to do now? Carry a gun?"

John slowly shook his head. "I don't know. Maybe."

He could see the suit reporter and the small woman were playing a twisted game of good cop/bad cop. "Montana doesn't need any more gunslingers out for vigilante justice, right, Mr. Urbain?" she asked.

Feeling tense, John said, "I do have a right to protect myself."

Now a slender man in his twenties, with a voice more feminine than John could stand, chimed in, "So you're going to go above the law, John?"

"Listen, you little shit: first, you can call me Mr. Urbain. Second, don't put words in my mouth."

The little shit shot back, "This city has a right to know, *Mr. Urbain*. I don't think you're a hero at all." The three other reporters all looked at the young snot with disapproving faces.

John stepped back, smiled. "I never tried to be." He slammed the door on them.

Ryan Porter said, moving the drapes slightly, "Looks like some of your neighbors want to be on TV."

"The hell with them all," John said, planting himself on his sofa. "What should I do? I feel I owe her justice."

"I don't know," Ryan said.

"I've got a splitting headache. Let me grab some aspirin," John said, rubbing his forehead. He still felt dizzy, but his headache was too much to handle without some relief. "I think I've got some in my bedroom," John said, heading down the hallway.

"Did you love her?" Ryan asked from the living room.

John stopped and turned around. "Yes." He felt an emptiness in his heart he had not known before.

In the bedroom, he sidestepped around the broken glass, sat on his bed, and opened the drawer to the nightstand.

Then he saw it: Longtree staring back at him with a grin. It was the picture he swiped from the pawnshop. He grabbed the picture and growled, "God help me. Ryan, come here!"

He heard him running down the hallway. "What's wrong?"

As he came into the room, John handed him the picture. "It's him. Longtree. I forgot about this damn photo." His heart sank as he looked at Ryan, who sat down next to him. "It's my fault she's dead. I should have given this to the police."

"I don't get it. Where…where did this come from?"

John told him about being at the pawnshop the day Detective Lewis was attacked and taking the picture. "Don't you see? It's got to be where he's hiding, in some shithole hunting cabin by Holter Dam." He snatched the photo away from Ryan. "If I would have shown the police this, Leann would still be alive."

"You don't know that. It's not your fault."

John's eyes were moist and he fell back on his bed. "No, it *is* my fault."

"So give it to them and be done with it," Ryan said, now standing.

"To what end?" John asked, sitting up quickly. "What if it was your wife? How could you just sit here, knowing Marie was murdered?"

"You're right. I'd want to kill him," Ryan said, punching his fists together, looking away.

John's anger was growing at a fever pitch. "What is right in our society? Do I obey the law or break it for what I consider the greater good? How and where do I draw the line?" He ran his hands through his hair. "It's a moral dilemma."

Ryan nodded in agreement and asked, "So what are you going to do? Play the vigilante role?"

"Why not? Longtree is running around free, and even if he is caught, some shady lawyer will plead insanity. There's no way he's going to spend the rest of his days getting three square meals a day with a shit-eating grin on his face, knowing he put one over on society, and my lovely lady in cold storage."

Ryan stood up, noticed the broken picture on the carpet, picked it up, and said with a smile, "Nice picture of you two. I've known you since you came to Skyway and consider you a good friend. I have to ask: What are you going to do?"

John caught a faint whiff of her perfume. He was glad the windows were closed. He wanted to hold onto her scent forever.

"I owe her justice. I can't let it go." He thought about his options for a moment, then continued, "I am not spending the rest of my days crying and wondering what might have been."

He pushed himself off the bed and clasped Ryan's shoulders. "I've got to find him. I think I may have an idea, but I'll need your help."

Looking over Ryan's shoulder to his open closet, John spotted his salvation hanging there. It was his olive-green Skyway Tours and Transport flight suit. It seemed to John there was a halo around it. He smiled, realizing it was only sunlight streaming through the window.

He took his flight suit off the hanger. Without looking at Ryan, he asked, "So you have off all day?"

"No, I have to be back soon to prep the Jet Ranger for a ride tomorrow at ten A.M. What are you thinking of doing?"

John laid the jumpsuit on his bed and, with a smile, said, "I'm thinking of borrowing the Jet Ranger and flying to his cabin to confront him."

Ryan slumped on the bed. "Borrow the Ranger! Are you crazy?"

John felt good; his headache slowly disappeared. He was inspired to flow into the dark side of his mind. "Why not? It's the quickest way to check and see if he's there." For the first time in a week he had a plan and direction he could live with. The consequences be damned.

"If he's not there, I'll fly back, face the crime head-on when they arrest me. At least I can say I tried."

The image of Annie Webster popped into John's mind. "What's Annie going to say?"

Ryan ran his hands through his dark hair. "You mean when she finds her Ranger has been stolen by a former employee searching the countryside for a murderer? Oh, I think she'll go ballistic on you, have you arrested, and throw away the key."

With a long smile, John replied, "So be it. Listen, just make sure the Jet Ranger is on the helipad, fueled up, and ready to go. Can you do that for me? I've got to try this, for Leann's sake."

John could see he was mulling it over. Ryan bit his lower lip and looked him in the eyes. "I'll do it only if I can come along."

John shook his head no. "I can't let you do it. If this all goes south, it will cost you your job, an arrest record, and worst of all, I'll have Marie on my ass," he said, laughing. "I'll climb the fence, do a quick preflight, and go before anyone finds out. I'll leave tomorrow around four-thirty, before sunrise. When you show up for work, try to give me some time before you call Annie and the police. I'll keep you out of it. We never had this conversation. Understand?" John could see Ryan was weakening to his demands.

Ryan stood up quickly. "If you find him and manage to kill him, you won't be able to come back. You'll be the wanted man now. Have you considered that?"

"I have." John looked out his bedroom window as the sun was just sinking behind the Rocky Mountains that he loved so much.

"My only focus is getting Longtree, dead or alive. Nothing else matters." He knew it would be the biggest gamble of his life.

42

John Urbain reached over and hit the alarm off button. He had set it for 2 A.M., but had lain awake for at least an hour or more. He lay there, thinking he probably wouldn't be back anytime soon. His face was splashed in the light from a full June moon streaming through his bedroom window.

With his hands laced behind his head, he went over his plan for the day. He still had a few minutes till he had to roll out of bed to begin the journey to find David Longtree. He said to himself, "Just take it one point at a time." He smiled. He felt good, considering he may not live to see tomorrow.

He blindly reached over to where Leann Blake should have been, only to feel the coolness of the sheets on his fingertips. He tried to smell again the faint perfume that she had worn. There was none to be found; the scent was gone forever.

He checked the time—1:59 A.M. "It's time," he muttered and jumped out of bed.

John shaved, showered, put on his olive-drab jumpsuit, and laced up his black military boots. He felt like a condemned man awaiting his last meal as he made black coffee and eggs with toast. He decided to let it all play out. If he found Longtree, he would try to take him alive, turning him over to law enforcement. If he had to, he would kill him, and then, John didn't know. He wondered if he would be the one on the run.

He poured himself a mug of coffee and studied the photo of Longtree's cabin: every tree, every rock, the framework of the cabin, and how it would appear from above. John knew the general area where the cabin was. They were few and far between, but he was sure he could find it. *The cabin has a dark red roof, which will help*, he thought.

He stuffed the photo in his front pocket, grabbed his coffee mug, and sat on his front steps. He shook his head as he saw, in his mind, the gunfight and kidnapping of Leann. He saw the sky was full of stars, and knew it would be a clear, blue-sky day. He could make out the sounds of insects and smelled the aroma of pine trees, letting it fill his nostrils one last time.

He walked around the garage to the grave of Prowler. He knelt down and placed his hand on the fresh mound.

John was now ready to leave.

As he drove on Interstate 15 towards Great Falls International Airport, he could see the bright lights off to the east from downtown. John wondered why he had never taken the time to explore its nightlife. Now he knew he never would have the chance.

He crossed over the Sun River with the exit to Airport Drive almost in sight. It hit him that he could not hide his pick-up. Everyone would know he was the one who stole the Bell Jet Ranger. "Fuck them," he muttered. John felt all of his senses were on heightened alert. Turning off the Interstate, he hoped Ryan had done his part.

Skyway Tours and Transport came into view at the north edge of the airport. He knew traffic to and from the airport would not heat up for at least an hour. Turning into Skyways' parking lot, his truck was bathed in floodlights. The lot was empty and would be till Ryan showed up at 5:30. His watch read 4:10; he had plenty of time.

Through the twelve-foot-high fence, he could see the Jet Ranger. "Thanks, Ryan." The medium-blue with black trim Bell 206L Jet Ranger was waiting for him like a chariot on the helipad.

He parked in the shadows, away from the glare of the lights. Looking up and down the fence line, he had to laugh. Annie Webster had not taken his advice for razor wire on top to prevent intrusion. He hurried to the fence line that spanned the sides of the building and tossed his overnight bag over. His heart was pounding as he scaled the wire fence, his shoulders ached. He straddled it, swung his legs, and jumped. With a thud he hit the pavement and rolled into the shadows.

His heart almost came through his chest as he saw an Airport Security vehicle cruise by on the flight line. John thought of all the felonies he was piling up. "Just let me get off the ground and clear the control tower," he said as he picked up his bag and ran towards the helicopter.

43

John Urbain kept his cool as he opened the door to the helicopter and tossed his overnight bag in. That's when he realized he was not alone.

"What the hell are you doing here?" he yelled at Ryan Porter in the co-pilot seat. "You can't go and I don't have time to debate the issue, now get out," John said, looking over his shoulder for airport security.

"Calm down, John. I talked it over with Marie, she's okay with it."

"Did you point out the fact you may be killed, and you're in a stolen helicopter?"

Ryan slowly smiled. "Well, no, I left that part out. Besides, you will need an extra set of eyes," he said, holding a pair of binoculars.

"You bastard. Don't make me regret doing this. Get out."

"Either we go together or not at all," Ryan said, folding his hands on his lap.

John shook his head, running both hands through his hair. "Then we go."

"Good," Ryan said with a satisfied smile, buckling the seat belt.

John took a deep breath and started the preflight around the outside of the helicopter as fast as he could.

He thought of all the possibilities of having Ryan tag along, most of them bad. John had to admit, an extra pair of eyes would help.

Finding the helicopter good to go, he climbed in and put his headset on.

John pointed to the headset. Ryan took note and put a pair on. John asked him to hand over the work log notebook.

"The helicopter is..."

Cutting him off, John said, "Do you mind if I see for myself?"

"Be my guest."

Making small talk, John asked, flipping the pages, "How did you get here?"

"Marie dropped me off. I told her I'd have a long day, nothing else."

"Let's hope we live to see tomorrow," John said.

One thing he could say about Ryan was he took excellent care of the helicopters he worked on. Everything had been fixed from the ambush.

From memory, John went through the steps to start the helicopter. He made sure not to skip or ignore any steps that could be fatal in flight. John checked the circuit breakers and warning lights, then pressed the starter button.

The main and tail rotors began to turn faster as he watched for red warning lights. The Jet Ranger was coming to life. All the gauges were in the green, where they should be. As the helicopter roared to full power, John looked over to Ryan. "Last chance, dude."

Ryan smiled. "Let's do it."

John turned the position beacon on to let the control tower know where they were.

Ryan asked, "Is that a good idea?"

John said, "The tower will not let me take off without it turned on. I'll switch it off when we reach Holter Dam."

"Sounds good."

"Hey, look at that," John said as a lone gray coyote was trotting across the runway and stopped in front of the helicopter. The coyote sat back on its hind legs and tilted its head with its tongue hanging out, watching them.

John smiled. The coyote's eyes reflected red from the overhead floodlights on Skyway's roof.

"Do you believe in omens?" Ryan asked, staring at the coyote.

"No, but we could use its cunning to find Longtree."

John went on, "Time to call the control tower and get the hell out of here."

He spoke into the microphone attached to his helmet. "Skyway 177 to Tower, asking for clearance."

After a moment they replied, "Tower to Skyway 177, where you heading at this hour?"

John's heart jumped a beat. What could he say?

"Is this John Urbain?" they asked.

Either way he was flying out of there, with or without clearance.

"I say again, is this John Urbain?" This time more forceful.

John looked over at Ryan, who was wide-eyed.

"Skyway 177 to Tower, yeah, it's me. Just testing some avionics equipment."

A full two minutes passed by. He was sure they were contacting airport security or calling Annie Webster.

With his hand over the mike, he asked Ryan, "Anybody let the Tower know I don't work here anymore?"

"I don't know," Ryan shot back.

"Tower to Skyway 177, at this hour?"

John was ready to say the hell with it, turn the helicopter into the wind, and split.

Gritting his teeth, he responded, "Skyway 177 to Tower, okay, you got me. I'm trying to pad some overtime hours."

They came back laughing, "We thought so. You are clear to proceed to west six-one-two runway. Have a safe flight."

John and Ryan both gave a thumbs-up signal.

John had to smile. There would be no laughing from the tower when they found out the helicopter was stolen. For now, he felt his blood pressure return to normal.

He looked, but the coyote was gone and Ryan shrugged his shoulders.

John leveled the helicopter in a hover at 20 feet, then made his way to west six-one-two runway.

He checked the time—5:02 A.M.

"Ryan, are you sure you're up for this? There's a huge chance you will lose your job. What about Marie and the kids?"

"Let me tell you something, my friend. We both know I am the best mechanic Annie has. Hell, I am one of the best in Montana. I've got money saved, I am not too worried about being unemployed. Besides, it's one hell of an adventure I would not want to miss," he said with a grin.

John looked over and said, smiling, "Just asking."

"I have to admit the look on Webster's face when she sees my pickup in the lot would be priceless," John went on.

Ryan turned towards him. "We'll be long gone by the time she shows up."

John eased the cyclic stick down with his right hand and adjusted the collective stick with his left, increasing the throttle. He pushed down with his right foot on the tail rotor pedals to bank right, and they were away.

His flight plan was simple: Fly west-southwest at 2,000 feet, then start a grid pattern expanding outward around Holter Dam.

"With any luck, we'll make Holter Dam in one hour doing around a hundred twenty knots. Not full speed, but close." He showed Ryan the picture of Longtree's cabin with the dark-red roof.

He didn't dare tell Ryan they had maybe two-and-a-half hours till police helicopters from around the state found their trail. With all the strategic missile sites scattered around Montana, would the police think he was a terrorist out to take control of a silo? Or would they call the big guns of F-18 fighters from the Air National Guard in Helena?

John cringed at the thought and tried to put the image of them being blown apart out of his head. There was no way he was going to let Ryan in on that thought, he decided.

Still, he smiled, the only person who knew where they were heading was sitting next to him. He looked over at Ryan and saw a faint trace of fear in his eyes.

Just maybe Leann Blake would watch over them. He was sure God would. *Let it play out. Let us return safely*, he prayed.

As John passed over the city of Ulm, he turned his attention to confronting David Longtree.

It was then that it hit him.

"Damn, how could I be so stupid?" John said in a calm voice, trying not to alarm Ryan.

"What's wrong?"

"Hold on a minute. Let me think," John said, scanning over the cockpit.

There was no weapon to be found. He had forgotten to pack one.

No way did he want to square off with Longtree empty-handed.

He needed some firepower. The only weapon he had, if you could call it one, was an old flare gun in the emergency bag stowed in the luggage compartment.

John thought of the bag Ryan had brought with him. "Any chance you have some firepower in that bag of yours?"

Ryan slowly turned towards John and smiled, reaching behind him for his bag. "Why yes, you could say that," he said with a coy smirk.

Reaching in his leather bag with both hands, he lifted out two twin .44 Magnum revolvers. "Fully loaded with extra ammo," he continued.

John peered over at Ryan. "You never cease to amaze me, dude."

Just maybe we can pull this off after all, John thought.

As he looked around at the cloudless blue sky, he could make out the city of Cascade up ahead. Below, Interstate 15 ran like a vein. Traffic was light for June, considering the out-of-state crowd on vacation.

His watch showed 5:40 A.M. John smiled; they were right on time.

"Do I have time for a quick nap?" Ryan asked with a yawn.

"Go ahead."

John took out his picture of himself and Leann, then thought better of it. This was not the time to go soft. He wanted to keep the fire burning for her. He still felt the rage inside and knew it would only increase as the day played out. For now, it was a controlled burn.

44

David Longtree had barely any sleep. He yawned as he sat on his kitchen floor in just his underwear. With a hammer and a crowbar, he pried up the floorboards one at a time till he had removed three of them. He reached in and almost forgot what he had in his private stash. There on top was a handheld grenade he won in a poker game from a retired Air Force supply sergeant. Next, he pulled out a dusty, loaded Smith & Wesson .45 with a box of shells. With both hands, he came across $4,000 in cash, all in hundreds and fifties. It was to be seed money for him and Tracy to start a new life somewhere.

David smiled. With the $2,200 he took off of Todd Rudd and Billy Ridge, it gave him enough to escape to Seattle. Lastly, there were energy bars in a leather bag with extra clothes.

His watch showed 5:50 A.M. Wednesday. He wanted to be on the road by 8 A.M. He was hoping to blend in with vacationers and out-of-state campers.

David was sure the state and local police would be out in force looking for him. The most direct route was west to Idaho, then on to Seattle. Canada would have been perfect, but no way did he want to endure its port of entry points. Mexico was too far to drive. *Maybe I could lose myself in Alaska*, he wondered. To top it off, there was no telling how the motor home would hold up driving in the mountains.

He cut his ponytail off, trimmed his long hair, and shaved. He washed up at the sink, put on a clean black t-shirt, blue jeans, and tennis shoes. The cabin was a mess, but what did it matter? He would not be coming back.

The thought of putting Billy's body in the cabin and torching it crossed his mind. David looked over his cabin. "The hell with it." He needed time and space to put between himself and the police. His guns were loaded and ready. No way he would be taken alive. Low profile was the name of this game.

He wanted to listen to Rudd's police scanner before leaving. He packed up all he had left—some money, guns, and not much else. From now on, the AK-47 was not going to leave his side.

He clipped the grenade to his belt.

45

John Urbain felt he was right on time as he flew over the town of Graig. He banked slightly to the right, following an unpaved road that led to Holter Dam in the distance. His watch read 6:10 A.M. Wednesday. At an altitude of 2,000 feet, he could make out the Gates of the Mountains Wilderness Area up ahead.

Rays of sunlight, like long fingers, were cast in hues of reddish-orange against the hills and buttes below. As he looked out, he marveled at the lush foliage below. *Montana is beautiful in June*, he thought.

He looked over at Ryan Porter, who was curled up asleep in the co-pilot's seat.

"Time to wake up."

Ryan almost jumped out of his seat. "What, where are we?"

"We're at Holter Dam. See if you can spot Longtree's cabin with those binoculars of yours."

"Right… My lights were out." Ryan grumbled, rubbing his eyes.

"Remember, we are looking for a dark-red-roofed hunting cabin. I'll start to expand the area in widening circles around the dam and climb to twenty-five hundred feet for a better view," John said. He felt like a hungry hawk out for prey. *Except this is no ordinary prey*, John thought. David Longtree had already tasted blood in Leann Blake's death. What was one more murder to him?

"We will find him," Ryan said, scanning the Montana landscape from side to side.

"Now let's see if we can find the little prick's lair," John said under his breath.

He hit every paved and unpaved road that was near Holter Dam. John flew over rivers, streams, through canyons, and down slopes to the prairie grass below.

It's got to be here, he thought.

"Anything?" he asked Ryan.

"Not yet."

Silently, John was feeling the pressure almost overwhelm him.

"There's plenty of homesteads and cabins, but I don't see any with a red roof," Ryan said.

John was thinking of the ramifications, then decided the hell with it and turned their position beacon to OFF. Instantly a warning light came on.

Ryan noticed the light. "Good thinking. We don't need anyone knowing where we are."

"But that tells the control tower we may have gone down," John said. "I'll have to call them or the sky will be filled with search-and-rescue aircraft," he continued.

It took a few minutes, but John convinced air traffic control that it was nothing more than a blown fuse. They wanted him to land immediately. John ignored the request.

"Annie's going to wonder where you and the helicopter are. You can expect a call," John said. "You might want to turn your cell phone off."

Ryan nodded.

John crossed over Interstate 15, then followed a bridge with the Missouri River below it.

Ryan leaned forward. "Hold it, what's that on your left? I see a dark-red-roofed cabin up ahead."

John's heart began pounding, realizing this must be the bridge where the love of his life was murdered. "Where?" John said, barely able to control himself.

"Next to that grove of pine and evergreen trees."

"I see it. I'll circle around," John said, adjusting the flight controls to bring the craft down to 100 feet.

"That's it. There's even that bastard Todd Rudd's van in the driveway," John said.

"Are you going to call it in to the police?" Ryan asked.

"No, you are," John said, looking over at him.

John's mind was already working on a plan; it did not involve Ryan.

"Let's see what we got here," he said. He could clearly see the cabin and long driveway. John's mouth went dry and his muscles tensed. He was ready to confront Longtree.

46

There was not a cloud in the sky but plenty of flies as David opened the back door to Rudd's van. He could feel the dry heaves coming on strong, viewing Billy Ridge's rotting body. With Billy's caved-in face and the stench of death surrounding David, he turned away and tried to vomit. But there was nothing in his stomach to bring up. It was twisted in knots. His mouth filled with bile. In between the heaves, he said, "Damn flies and maggots."

He put his hands on his knees, bent over, and tried to maintain himself. His head hurt, even after downing four aspirin an hour ago.

David wondered if there was anything he had forgotten to pack before he left.

No, the motor home was ready to go.

He grabbed his AK-47 that was leaning against the van. It was locked and loaded. He felt better knowing the machine gun was next to him.

He opened all the doors to the van, hoping to air it out before he climbed in to use the police scanner.

David took a deep breath and crawled in. "The hell with the smell," he said to himself. He laid his AK-47 on the dash and turned on the scanner.

David was anxious to hear what law enforcement had to say this morning. He made himself as comfortable as he could and tried to stay awake. His eyelids were heavy; his head drooped with useless police chatter on the scanner. He faded in and out of sleep till he heard his name.

"Be on the lookout for one David Samuel Longtree, wanted in connection with first-degree murder and kidnapping. Approach with extreme caution. Last seen driving a late-model van with…"

David turned it off. He had heard enough.

It was then his ears picked up the faint wash of helicopter blades moving closer.

Without thinking, he grabbed the machine gun, jumped out of the van, and sought cover under a large evergreen spruce tree.

The sound was to his left and becoming louder. Could it be the police?

David turned, but could not see it through the thick foliage.

He knew if it was the police and they spotted Rudd's van, he would be screwed. Law enforcement from all over would swarm on him faster than the maggots on Billy's face. No way did he want to die here. He flicked the safety off on his machine gun.

David lay down flat and waited for the helicopter to pass overhead. He was covered in needles and cones. He still felt sick. Now he was sweating from his head.

For no reason, the image of Carl, his older brother, popped into his mind.

David wondered if this was how Carl had suffered as the police closed in on him.

Alone. Hiding like an animal.

David shook his head quickly, bringing himself back to reality. He noticed his hands were shaking. He took a deep breath, flexing his fingers.

"Son of a bitch," he yelled as the helicopter passed over. Clearly whoever it was had found Rudd's van, he thought.

"No use hiding anymore." He backed out from under the evergreen and stood up.

David still was not sure who it was, the police or maybe the F.B.I. He took aim at the tail rotors with the machine gun with its 30-round clip.

He knelt down and flicked his AK-47 to full automatic. Before he could fire, the helicopter disappeared behind a pile of large boulders ten feet high and 40 feet wide at the end of his driveway.

His head was spinning as he broke out running towards the rocks. He was breathless as he reached the boulders and felt dizzy.

David crept slowly around the left side and then crouched down to rest.

He peeked around the boulders till the front of the helicopter was in view. The blades were turning slowly, but there was no pilot.

It was then he saw the markings.

I don't believe it. It's him, the A-hole from the ambush. Where'd he go?

David was stunned and weak-kneed. It was not the police, but a Skyway Tours and Transport craft.

The prick who took Tracy Burke from me, he thought.

His blood was boiling. "Show yourself, you bastard!"

He took aim at what he guessed was the fuel tank, then lowered his weapon.

David had something else in mind. He smiled.

He backed up around the boulders and unclipped the grenade from his belt.

47

"After I set her down, make a run for those boulders, got it?"

Ryan looked down, then nodded. John could sense Ryan's heart was not into this; he was too quiet.

"My gut tells me Longtree is close, and I am sure he'll have that Russian heater by his side. Time to lock and load," John added.

He landed the helicopter with ease behind the wall of boulders.

After shutting her down and making sure his Magnum was loaded and the safety was off, he bolted towards a huge crevice in the wall with Ryan behind him.

"Let me have a handful of shells," he said to Ryan, who looked scared and out of place.

Ryan fumbled with the box and said, "I can't do this, I can't..."

"Don't worry about it," John said, trying to keep him calm. "Stay with the helicopter. If I am not back in one hour, call it in, okay?"

Ryan nodded but kept his head down.

"I forgot my gun," Ryan said, standing up. Before John could warn him of Longtree, he ran off towards the helicopter.

"Get down!" John shouted after him. In an instant there was a flash of light, then a massive explosion with a shockwave that kicked John like a wild mule. He went shoulder first into the boulders and lost his balance but managed to protect his head. John passed out for a few seconds.

When he became alert, his left shoulder ached and his ears were ringing. That's when he noticed a huge plume of black smoke and flames that obscured the sun.

The helicopter was engulfed.

He looked around and tried to find Ryan amongst the strewn wreckage.

John stepped out from behind the rocks; then he saw him. Ryan was lying in a twisted heap not more than ten feet away against the rocks. He was either dead or out cold.

John ran to him and gently felt for a heartbeat underneath his jumpsuit.

"Thank God," John said as he found a heartbeat, a little weak but beating. "Can you hear me?" he said loudly.

Ryan stirred slightly, his eyes blinking.

John was afraid he would lapse into a coma. John lightly shook him and asked again, "Can you hear me?"

Ryan's eyes fluttered, then opened wide. "What the hell happened?"

"I don't know, but something hit the fuel tank," John said, looking at the burning rubble. He could smell burnt plastic and kerosene oil among the flames.

"Can you move?" he asked Ryan.

"I don't think so. Part of the engine cowling hit me, and I fell against the boulders. I'm sure my right wrist is broken and my knees hurt."

John could see Ryan's wrist was swelling up. "I'm going to move you to a safe place, okay?"

"Go ahead," Ryan said as a small amount of blood trickled from his mouth.

John grabbed Ryan under the arms from behind, slowly backing him away from the smoke and flames.

Once Ryan was safe, he told him, "Just try to relax. I'll be back as soon as I can. This smoke is bound to attract the police. Hang in there. I've got to find Longtree and end this crap."

John drew his .44 Magnum, kept low, and made his way around the edge of the boulders to the long driveway.

There in the distance was David Longtree, jogging towards a large brown motor home.

"Hey, Longtree," John yelled and took aim at his head.

John could see David turn towards his voice and fire a burst before disappearing into the motor home.

The distance was too far for John to have taken a clean shot.

He took off running towards the motor home. There was no way John would let him escape again. He had to get to the back of that motor home and somehow jump on.

48

He was unsure whether the grenade would work. If it did, he was going to blow the helicopter sky high. David Longtree hastily pulled the pin and tossed it underneath the helicopter. He ducked down behind a large boulder in time to hear the explosion.

After a few seconds he peeked around the boulder and saw the towering plume of smoke and flames, smiling from ear to ear.

Then the full impact of what he had done hit him. This was going to draw the police big time. He picked up his AK-47 and slowly eyed his surroundings, still not sure where John Urbain was. He could see the motor home was about 150 feet away.

He backed away from the rocks, keeping his machine gun at eye level with a finger on the trigger.

If I can just make it to the motor home.

He swung the gun from side to side, slowly backing away from the wall of rocks. He was now in the open with no sign of Urbain.

"The hell with it." He turned and took off, running zig-zag towards the motor home.

David heard his name being called. Without thinking he turned, saw Urbain, and fired a quick burst.

"Bastard fuck," he said to himself.

The motor home was only ten feet away. *I made it.*

David grabbed the door handle, almost ripping it from its hinges, and rushed in.

He placed the machine gun in the passenger seat and jumped into the driver's chair. He had only seconds to scan the dash. David turned the key, fired the engine, and shifted into gear in one smooth motion. He punched the gas pedal. He had to back out of his long driveway.

David looked to the outside mirrors. Seeing no one, he smiled.

He took the .45 off the dash, placing it between his legs. He felt secure, and the machine gun at his side made him laugh.

The motor home gained speed. David turned sharply to avoid the potholes.

If I can just reach the damn paved road, I am home free.

Still, with a helicopter burning out of control in his yard, he would need some major luck to escape. *I might die today, but I am going to take as many as I can with me straight to hell.*

49

With each step John Urbain dug his heels deeper in loose gravel, running all out. The motor home was pulling away. He abruptly stopped and took aim at the front tires.

John dropped to one knee, fired three rounds. “Damn,” he shouted.

His right arm ached from the gun kickback. He could only watch as the motor home made the end of the driveway.

“No way, no damn way.” John had to think fast. *What now?*

He saw Todd Rudd’s van and took off.

John tripped on a pothole and landed hard, ripping his jumpsuit at the knees. He limped over to Rudd’s van and looked in. *Luck is on my side.* Keys were left in the ignition.

“What the hell is that smell?” he said, fanning flies from his face. He looked in the back and felt a rush of vomit he was barely able to hold down, not only from the dead body but the knowledge that this was the very place where Leann had lain only hours before.

“Oh my God,” he said, holding his nose. “I don’t have time to sort this out now.” He slammed the doors, ran around to the front, and flung himself behind the wheel.

He turned the key. The engine sounded as if it was about to flood, then it growled to life in blue exhaust smoke.

He jammed the shift lever into reverse and said to the corpse in back, “Hold on, old man, here we go.” *This is pure insanity. Now I am talking to dead people.*

John's mind was nothing but fireworks and pinwheels. He could not think, only react.

The van stunk of death and flies.

He drove backwards around the potholes faster than he wanted, almost losing control.

John whipped the wheel to the right at the end of the driveway. He made the turn onto the paved road and looked back. The helicopter was still burning down to the metal frame.

He hoped Ryan had not passed out, or worse.

He jammed it into drive and floored the gas pedal.

Longtree was nowhere in sight, but that big brown motor home would be a bitch to hide. *I'll find him. I've got to.*

John could only manage a top speed of 60 with a cloud of blue smoke trailing behind him. He cleared a hill, then saw the motor home winding around a bend in the road.

"There you are, you little prick," he said spitting out the window.

John was tense, like a heavyweight boxer entering the ring. His mind was clear now.

Blood revenge is the best healer, he thought.

John quickly reviewed the events of the past week in his mind. All he could do was shake his head in disbelief. He felt he had aged ten years without Leann.

Who in the hell is the old man with the caved-in face? he wondered.

He could clearly see Longtree once he rounded the bend. John had closed the gap to less than a quarter mile. He kept the pedal floored as he prayed the engine would hold out. The white lines on the highway blurred to a single line. He felt the engine shudder. "Hold on, damn you, don't fail me now!"

John began to rock back and forth in his seat in an effort to will the van faster. He had no idea where he was. There was only barren open areas, scrub grass, and tumbleweeds, interlaced with buttes and prairie flowers.

The gap closed to 30 feet. *If I can only get around him.*

He swung the van into the passing lane, his eyes opened wide to oncoming death. He jerked the wheel back in time to hear the horn blaring from a blue station wagon just missing the van. John screamed in horror at the top of his lungs. He was white-knuckled and full of fury.

"Take this, Longtree, let's play!" John said, ramming his bumper into the motor home. Nothing. He had to force the motor home off the road somehow.

He slowed down enough to get a clear view of its back tires. John had to shoot the tires out. There was no other way. John pointed his .44 Magnum out the window and fired. His hand jerked back from the force, but he held on.

He knew he had only two shots left till he had to reload.

"Help me, Leann," he said, praying. He aimed the best he could and fired.

A cloud of smoke from a blown tire told John he hit the mark.

The motor home swerved back and forth with chunks of rubber exploding from the rim. John smiled slightly. He had hit the left inside tire of a four-tire axle. The motor home was slowing down. "There's nowhere to run, Longtree, it ends here." John aimed and fired again, this time taking out the left outside tire.

Now he'll have to stop, John thought as he ran over bits of rubber.

The motor home veered left, crashing down on its left axle. In a billow of smoke and sparks, the axle was now digging into the pavement.

John slowed down. He could afford to wait now. Longtree had to stop sooner or later. John kept the steering wheel between his knees as he reloaded.

The motor home abruptly slid sideways on the road, then stopped.

John hit the brakes and came to a halt 10 feet away.

John looked up at the motor home's driver side window. Their eyes met. He got out of the van, firing a round at the window, shattering it.

Running to the window, John fired two more as Longtree, with one hand, sprayed rounds from the AK-47, hitting John in the right leg.

With intense pain, John dropped to the pavement, rolling underneath the motor home. At least if Longtree came out, John could shoot at his legs. Longtree was trapped in the motor home.

John checked his wound. There was no doubt about it, he would pass out from loss of blood. He reloaded as fast as he could with bloody hands. He had to end this now.

He wiped sweat from his eyes, then had an idea.

John yelled, “Give it up, Longtree, or die in there.”

From somewhere inside, he got his reply. “Fuck off and die.”

The smell of burnt rubber almost caused John to pass out. He had to find the gas tanks and burn him out.

Lying on his back, he opened his jumpsuit to his waist, took off his t-shirt, and tried to secure his wound with it. He yelled in pain as his right leg went numb.

John slowly crawled to the back of the underside of the motor home. He found what he was looking for: fuel tanks.

He continued to crawl till he was in the open with his back against the rear of the motor home.

“Hey, Longtree, why did you do it?”

John kept his eyes on the back window, backing away.

“What?” came the curt reply.

“The ambush, the killings, everything,” John said, taking aim at the tanks.

“Love, money, fame. As far as that bitch goes, I enjoyed it, old man.”

“For that, you will die.” John fired four shots at the fuel tanks. “You little prick,” John said as the tanks ruptured, spewing gasoline.

It was then that Longtree opened the drapes to the window. Longtree took aim at John.

John took out his spare book of matches he kept in his jumpsuit for emergencies. He smiled and moved to the right side of the motor home before Longtree could fire.

He lit the whole book with his bloody hands and tossed it on the saturated pavement. There was a swift rush of combustion, then ignition, followed by intense heat that knocked John to the ground. The motor home exploded in smoke and flames.

John backed away like a wounded crab dragging one leg. He bit his lip and endured the sharp pain from his wound as he sought safety.

He found himself facing the only door into the motor home. He took aim and he waited for Longtree to emerge. "This is for you, Leann. Sleep easy, babe," John said.

The flames licked higher up the motor home, now swallowed up.

"Come out now, Longtree, and face your justice!"

"See you in hell," came the reply.

Then, only a single gunshot from inside the motor home told John all he needed to know.

John Urbain dropped his gun and dragged his worn body over to the side of the road. He fell to his knees. Looking towards the sun, he thought he saw helicopter blades cutting the rays of light.

He lost it.

Then only darkness.

THE END